The Bumper LITERATURE QUIZ

Berty Ashley is a molecular biologist with the Dystrophy Annihilation Research Trust and works with rare genetic disorders. What is not rare though is to see him conducting quizzes or attending them. He is the author of the popular *Easy Like Sunday Morning* series of quizzes published in *The Hindu Sunday* magazine. Berty is also a lover of music—not only playing but collecting, as is evident by his growing stack of vinyl records of Jazz, Prog, Hindustani and Heavy metal music. He and his partner, Akhila, live in Bengaluru, surrounded by books, music, and an assortment of pens and guitars.

Akhila Phadnis is a freelance translator. She holds a Masters in Translation Studies from Durham University, UK, and in Psychology from Madras University, Chennai, Tamil Nadu. She enjoys reading, practising calligraphy, learning new languages, quizzing, board games, and taking long walks by the beach.

The Bumper LITERATURE QUIZ

BERTY ASHLEY
AND
AKHILA PHADNIS

RUPA

Published by
Rupa Publications India Pvt. Ltd 2019
7/16, Ansari Road, Daryaganj
New Delhi 110002

Sales centres:
Allahabad Bengaluru Chennai
Hyderabad Jaipur Kathmandu
Kolkata Mumbai

ISBN: 978-93-5333-597-7

First impression 2019

10 9 8 7 6 5 4 3 2 1

The moral right of the author has been asserted.

CONTENTS

Introduction   *vii*

1. Children's Literature I   1
2. Comic Books and Magazines   9
3. Children's Literature 2   16
4. Ancient Literature   23
5. Biographies and Autobiographies   28
6. Historical and Political Literature   37
7. Plays and Dramas   42
8. Poetry   47
9. Indian Literature in English   53
10. Indian Literature in the Vernacular   58
11. Fiction   63
12. Science Fiction   72
13. Detective and Hero Novels   80
14. Fantasy and Graphic Novels   88
15. Spin the Colour Wheel   95
16. Printing and Publishing   102

Acknowledgements   109

INTRODUCTION

Why books? Why quizzes?

Books have played an integral part in both our lives. Some of our deepest friendships formed over a shared book and our earliest memories involve school libraries. Although we both went to different schools, we were both very lucky in having had great librarians who encouraged any child with an interest in books to explore the library and read widely.

Books give you a whole host of pleasures: information, magical new worlds, new friends, and characters you care about deeply (or characters that annoy you till you sympathize with anyone else in the book who expresses the same annoyance!). More than anything else, they provide you with a rich inner world, while allowing you to express yourself more easily in the language you read in. Book lovers are also self-sufficient, easily-entertained and satisfied.

Where does quizzing fit in? Quizzing is nothing more than examining a piece of information from a different angle and using any clues you know to piece together an answer. Books are great material and fodder for the avid quizzer! It's impossible for anyone to have read every book of significance in the world (despite all the 'BOOKS YOU MUST READ' lists that constantly float around!), but you pick up enough information about them just from hearing teachers, peers and the media discussing these books. These kinds of books feature in this quizbook, books that are so widely discussed that even people who have never read them are familiar with them. But we've also included books that many people are highly likely to have read in school and college, providing you with new nuggets of information or an angle you might not have considered before!

We hope that through this book, various book lovers and even those who don't consider themselves book lovers or 'bookish' can derive hours of entertainment, piecing together the clues and cracking the questions or, perhaps, learning a new fact every day.

We recommend quizzing in groups or even by yourself during long commutes or when you want a break from work or study. Wherever and in whatever way you quiz yourself and others, we hope you enjoy yourselves thoroughly.

Finally, books and quizzes have played a major role in how we met each other and eventually combined our eclectic and ever-growing book collections into one even more eclectic and ever-growing collection. We hope that in the course of reading and quizzing, readers of this book may also find new friends or deepen existing friendships while discussing some little 'TIL' (*Today I Learnt*) from the book!

1. CHILDREN'S LITERATURE I

1. At present, this book is available in well over 50 editions in English, including versions in verse, audiobooks, films, picture books, pop-up books, knitting patterns, graphic novels and scholarly annotated editions. The musical adaptation in 2016 was the first London West End musical to raise £1 million through crowdfunding. The book is not considered to be an animal story as it is supposed to be about humans and the tree mentioned in the title does not appear in the book even once! Which is this book that has nothing to do with childhood or children, except that it can be enjoyed by the young?

2. Carlo Lorenzini translated French fairy tales into Italian. He wrote a book called *Storiadiun Burattino* (The Story Of a Marionette), also called *Le Avventuredi_____*, which was published as a weekly in *Il Giornale De Bambini*, one of Italy's first newspapers for children. There are multiple film adaptations of this book in multiple languages, an asteroid named after it, and the title character was used as the mascot for the 2013 UCI Road World Championships.

Lorenzini died, unaware of the fame and popularity of his work. Which book is this?

3. Jenny Lind was an opera soprano. In 1843, this author met her and fell in love with her. Lind, however, treated him as a friend. She served as the inspiration for some of his stories, especially 'The Nightingale'. In this story, a nightingale is replaced by a mechanical bird. When the bird begins to malfunction from overuse, the owner of the bird begins to die from the lack of music. On what would have been the last night of his life, the nightingale returns and sings a song to keep death at bay, and the owner recovers. Who was this smitten author?

4. In 1841, New Yorkers waited for news from Europe concerning the fate of 'Little Nell'. Her 'death' was greeted by shock on both sides of the Atlantic, especially in the United States. This was one of the first times that the 'death' of a fictional character affected people on such a large scale. However, unlike with the 'death' of Sherlock Holmes over Reichenbach Falls, 'Little Nell' did not come back. Name the author who created 'Little Nell' and the book she appeared in.

5. These are the first lines of a poem called 'The Solitude of Alexander Selkirk' by William Cowper. This was based on the real-life story of Selkirk, a Scottish Naval Officer.

I am monarch of all I survey,
My right there is none to dispute;
From the centre all round to the sea,
I am lord of the fowl and the brute.

It inspired a book that has multiple film adaptations,

including one where a FedEx employee ends up having a volleyball for a friend. Name the book.

6. This book is notable for the author's unromantic portrayal of criminals and their sordid lives. The book exposed the cruel treatment of many a waif-child in London, which increased international concern in what is sometimes known as The Great London Waif Crisis. The book calls the public's attention to various contemporary evils, including child labour, the recruitment of children as criminals and the presence of street children. The novel's serious themes are written with sarcasm and dark humour. The novel may have been inspired by the story of Robert Blincoe, an orphan whose account of hardships as a child labourer in a cotton mill was widely read in the 1830s. It is likely that the author's own early youth as a child labourer contributed to the story's development. Name the novel and the author.

7. *The Land of Far-Beyond* is a 1942 children's novel written by Enid Blyton. It's about a boy named Peter and his two sisters, Anna and Patience, who travel from the City of Turmoil carrying the heavy burdens of their bad deeds on their backs. He who places these burdens on them tells them that to get their burdens removed, they must walk to the City of Happiness in the Land of Far-Beyond without being tempted away from the straight, narrow and dangerous path that is the only way to their destination. During their journey, they meet characters named Kindly, Daring, Bold and Friendly, as well as others named Cruelty, Misery, Poverty and Pain. This book is based on a Christian allegory written in 1678 which also forms the basis of the brilliant concept album

The Similitude of a Dream by the Neal Morse Band. What is the original book?

8. Samuel Clemens purchased his Remington typewriter in 1874 for a then princely sum of $125. At first, he wanted to get rid of it as he thought it corrupted his morals, because it made him want to swear. But he eventually laboured on. Two years later, his most famous work was published about a boy of about 12 years of age, who resides in the fictional town of St. Petersburg, Missouri, in the year 1845. He released it under a pseudonym which refers to the second mark on the line that measured the safe depth (12 ft) for a steamboat. Though it's not conclusively proven, this is supposed to be the first ever novel written on a typewriter. Which novel is this that is found in pretty much all school libraries?

9. India is the only country in the world that has both lions and tigers in the wild. The species are likely to have met each other earlier, but by the 1800s this was no longer likely, since lions had been wiped out from tiger habitats by then. At that time, tigers numbered up to 100,000 in the wild. Eventually, due to hunting, poaching and habitat loss, their numbers dwindled. Lions lived in the dry deciduous savannah, whereas tigers lived in the dense thick forests which were more prevalent in India. The Bengal tiger has always been the most feared predator of the wild forests, with one of the places it is found being the Seoni area in Madhya Pradesh. All of these reasons contributed to why a certain author chose a certain character as the villain of his book. Can you name the character and the author?

10. American novelist Daniel Handler is the author of

several children's books but is well known for a series written under a pseudonym. In the series, he is the narrator and also a character. As a character, he is a troubled writer and photographer falsely accused of felonies. He is continuously hunted by the police and his enemies, the fire-starting side of the secret organization, Volunteer Fire Department. He falls in love with a girl but before they can get married, he is falsely reported dead and she marries another person and has children with him. Unfortunately the couple die, leaving behind the three children. The character then feels obliged to chronicle their lives, which is the main subject of thirteen novels. What is the citrusy-sounding name of the author/character? What is the name of the series?

11. In 1945, E.B. White, best known then as a contributor to *The New Yorker* and co-author of *Elements of Style*, published his first children's book. The lead character, who acted very much like a rat, had appeared to him in a dream. The book had a long incubation period and it was White's wife and friends who encouraged him to continue with it and get it published. The book has now become a children's classic and one of the earliest reviewers said this about it: 'Mr White has a tendency to write amusing scenes instead of telling a story. To say that _____ is one of the best children's books published this year is very modest praise for a writer of his talent.' Fill in the blanks.

12. Astrid Lindgren is among the top five most-translated children's authors (according to the UNESCO translation index). Although she wrote a large number of books for children, her best-known series is that featuring a spirited

young girl who lives alone with a horse and monkey (her father is off at sea), has superhuman strength and defies the rules that adults try to set. Generations have loved this girl, who was created when Lindgren's daughter wanted a story while at home recovering from an illness. Her name in the original Swedish is _____lotta Viktualia Rullgardina Krusmynta Efraimsdotter Långstrumpor, as she is usually known, _____Långstrump. The English name is a direct translation of the Swedish one. Who is this entertaining and kind-hearted child whose antics have delighted generation after generation?

13. This American novelist is thought to have transformed the genre of family stories for children when, in 1868–69, she published her novel about four sisters in Civil War America and also wrote sequels to this novel, focusing on the later lives of the sisters and their families. However, despite this being her most famous book, the author herself saw it as a formulaic book and seems to have derived greater pleasure from writing 'sensational' short stories featuring independent and empowered women who choose their own destinies (written under the pseudonym A.M. Barnard). Even in her famous book, where the second sister was modelled on herself, it was only due to social and publishing conventions that her character got married and had a family. This book has inspired multiple film and television versions. Name the author and the book.

14. This collection of fables is supposed to be among the most widely-translated texts of all time. It was translated from Sanskrit into Persian sometime in the sixth century CE and travelled across many other languages through

the centuries. The twelfth-century Hebrew translation became the definitive version from which most European translations were derived. The book is supposed to be a collection of stories narrated by a wise scholar to educate the three dim-witted sons of a powerful king, to help them become powerful rulers. What is its original Sanskrit name, which refers to the five chapters or texts that make up the collection of stories?

15. *Roverandom* is a novella about the adventures of a young dog that is turned into a toy by an irritable wizard, and then goes in search of the wizard to get him to reverse the spell. The story was written for the author's youngest son, Michael, who was upset over the loss of his toy dog. The story was submitted for publication in 1937, following the success of the author's previous book. However, it was only published 60 years later. While the story is a departure from the kind of work the author is most famous for, an irritable and powerful wizard is not a new character in his tales! Who is this author?

ANSWERS

1. *The Wind in the Willows*
2. *Pinocchio*
3. Hans Christian Andersen
4. *The Old Curiosity Shop*, Charles Dickens
5. *Robinson Crusoe*
6. *Oliver Twist*, Charles Dickens
7. *Pilgrim's Progress*
8. *Tom Sawyer*

9. Shere Khan; the tiger from *The Jungle Book*, Rudyard Kipling
10. Lemony Snicket, *A Series of Unfortunate Events*
11. *Stuart Little*
12. Pippi Longstocking
13. *Little Women*, Louisa May Alcott
14. *Panchantantra*
15. J.R.R. Tolkien

'Outside of a dog, a book is man's best friend. Inside of a dog, it's too dark to read.'

—Groucho Marx

2. COMIC BOOKS AND MAGAZINES

1. 'Acquired growth hormone deficiency and hypogonadotropic hypogonadismin a subject with repeated head trauma' or 'X goes to the neurologist' was a research paper published in the *Canadian Medical Association Journal* in 2004. It describes the unique case of a public figure that is well known for having delayed pubertal development and statural growth. It is believed that the researchers have discovered why X, a young reporter whose stories were published between 1929 and 1975, never grew taller and never needed to shave. The research team successfully identified 50 significant losses of consciousness. Of these, 43 incidents involved head trauma with loss of consciousness representing grade 3 concussions. X sustained 26 concussions resulting from a blow with a blunt object. The most frequently used object was a club (8 times). Other causes for the subject's loss of consciousness included bullet injury (3), chloroform poisoning (3), explosions (4), car accidents (3) and falls (2). Who is X, who often escapes from these harrowing

situations thanks to his faithful canine companion?

2. This character from a popular comic book series mostly teaches chemistry and occasionally also teachers other subjects such as music and astronomy. He has tufts of curly white hair at his temples but is otherwise bald and has a long, thin nose. Only his surname is mentioned; it comes from his nose and resembles a musical instrument. The name comprises of the name of the instrument and an old American slang word for a nose. What is the name of this character?

3. Anthea Bell was born in 1936. She specialized in translating children's literature, and retranslated Hans Christian Andersen's fairy tales from Danish to English. Other books and comic series translated by her include *Le Petit Nicolas, Lieutenant Blueberry* and *Iznogoud*. She has either won, or been honourably mentioned, for the most number of Mildred L. Batchelder Awards, which is awarded by the American Library Association to recognize each year's 'most outstanding' children's book translated into English. Along with Derek Hockridge, which highly popular comic series is she most renowned for, especially for the excellent puns which kept the spirit of the original French humour intact?

4   This comic series was started by a gentleman when he realized, during a Doordarshan quiz in 1967, that the students could answer questions about Greek and Roman mythology but were ignorant about Indian mythology and folklore. He left his work at *The Times of India* and started the now-popular comic book series for which he was writer, editor and publisher. The series went on to sell over 100 million copies of about 440 titles. The

name of the series means 'immortal picture stories' and is available in 20 Indian languages. What is the name of this series?

5. The editor and the associate editor of the series in the above question were discussing the creation of a new comic for children. The editor wanted a musical name for this comic and they were discussing the options when the phone rang and interrupted them. After disconnecting the call, the associate editor, Mr Subba Rao, realized that he had the name. His editor and the team approved it, leading to the creation of one of India's most beloved comics for children, which is still going strong. Name the comic.

6. This is a children's fortnightly magazine which was first published in 1969. It has three colourful sections: Stories, Picture Stories and Your Page. It has modern stories with a moral tone for children. Currently, it is available in eight languages. What is this comic magazine which is named after an evergreen tree of the magnolia family with orange flowers?

7. John X was an influential French theologian, pastor and reformer during the Protestant Reformation. X was a tireless writer of polemic and defences of Christinaity, who generated quite a lot of controversy. Thomas Y was an English philosopher who is considered one of the founders of modern political philosophy. Y developed some of the fundamentals of liberal thought, such as the right of the individual, the natural equality of all men, and his understanding of humans as being matter and motion, obeying the same physical laws as other matter and motion, remains influential. These two names were

given new life by a comic artist who was working in an advertising job he detested. What are their names that you would come across if you read any one of the 2,400 newspapers or 45 million copies of the books they have been in?

8. This comic strip character is the personal safety mascot for all NASA space missions. This unlikely partnership came about after the Apollo 1 fire, when NASA approached the creator for permission and he said yes. This character was chosen because he had a long history of dreaming of flight and usually envisioned himself in a biplane in a dogfight. Since 1968, a small silver metal pin depicting the character with a fishbowl helmet is sent with every astronaut and on return it is given to the people who worked hard to keep these astronauts safe. Who is this character that you would usually see lying on top of his house, dreaming?

9. William Moulton Marsh's doctoral thesis in 1921 was titled 'Systolic Blood Pressure Symptoms of Deception and Constituent Mental States.' Basically, by testing a subject's systolic blood pressure, one would be able to determine whether the subject was lying or telling the truth. This was the basis for the lie-detector machine (polygraph). Marsh, along with his wife, Elizabeth, and their partner, Olive Byrne, were also responsible for the creation of a superhero who, along with superpowers, also has the Lasso of Hestia which forces anyone it captures to tell the truth, a bit like the polygraph machine. Which superhero wields this lasso?

10. This is a fortress located on the fictional planet of Eternia. It has been described as once being the beautiful Hall of

Wisdom, the 'centre of Eternian culture and a storehouse of all knowledge of the universe'. The Hall was the meeting place of the Council of Elders. The elders concentrated all of their power into a magical orb and magically transformed the Hall of Wisdom into this fortress in order to frighten away intruders and protect the orb. Man-at-Arms eventually led Prince Adam to X, where Prince Adam transformed into the being we know him better as. What is the name of the fortress and who is X?

11. This red-haired, freckled character is the mascot of a long-running magazine. He made his debut on the cover in 1954, and just two years later, 'ran' for US presidency. Every now and then during election he is reoffered as a candidate with the slogan 'You could do worse... and always have!' In 2005, Hillary Clinton remarked 'I sometimes feel that (character name) is in charge in Washington', referring to George W. Bush's 'What, me worry?' attitude. Which American humour magazine's mascot is this character?

12. This fictional character has a symbol for a middle name. Since the first issue in 1960, the character had a run of 254 issues, making him the most popular series of an American comic book company Harvey Comics. Despite the possible negative stereotypes associated with his status, he is portrayed as kind and charitable. He has a faithful dog who, instead of being covered in spots, is covered in the symbols that also make up his master's middle name. This leads to a neat pun on the breed of dog he actually is. Who is this lovable character who has inspired many films and franchises, and what breed is his dog?

13. This supposedly Scottish character, named after a Charles Dickens character, is a self-proclaimed 'adventure-capitalist' with a very thrifty attitude. He was initially supposed to be an antagonist to his nephew, but got so popular that he became a co-adventurer and soon had a comic book series for himself which started in 1952 and continues to run. He is also the person whose signature is on all the currency used in the amusement park which is centred around his universe. What is this character's name and who is his nephew?

14. This was a comic strip created by Chester Gould about a tough and intelligent police detective who uses forensic science, advanced gadgetry and wits in an early example of the police procedural mystery story. First seen in 1931, Gould animated the strip which ran till 1977 when he retired, after which various artists have taken over. In 1980, the Mystery Writers of America honoured Gould and his work with a Special Edgar Award, making it the first such win ever for a comic strip. What is the name of the comic strip and the name of the detective?

15. In 1870, a German chemist calculated the amount of iron found in different vegetables. When publishing his findings, he accidentally left out a decimal point for one particular vegetable and instead of '3.5 mg per 100 g' he wrote '35 mg'. This started a myth about this vegetable that even gave birth to a popular comic character who had a passion for this vegetable. Which vegetable's history in pop culture is based on this misinformation and what is the name of the comic character?

ANSWERS

1. Tintin
2. Mr Flutesnoot; from *Archie* comics
3. *Asterix* comics
4. *Amar Chitra Katha*
5. *Tinkle*
6. *Champak*
7. Calvin and Hobbes
8. Snoopy; from *Peanuts*
9. Wonder Woman
10. Castle Grayskull, He-Man
11. *Mad Magazine*
12. Richie. $. Rich, Dollarmatian
13. Scrooge McDuck, Donald Duck
14. Dick Tracy
15. Spinach, Popeye the Sailorman

'When I look back, I am so impressed again with the life-giving power of literature. If I were a young person today, trying to gain a sense of myself in the world, I would do that again by reading, just as I did when I was young.'
—Maya Angelou

3. CHILDREN'S LITERATURE 2

1. In 1987, Anne Fine published a book about a family where the parents are divorced and the father wants to spend more time with his three children. This book was turned into a film in 1993, starring the late Robin Williams, and three years later, was also adapted into an Indian film starring Kamal Haasan. What was the name of the book (which was modified slightly in the name of the 1993 film)?

2. This famously reclusive author's first name was Nelle, which was her grandmother's name spelt backwards. She wrote a Pulitzer-prizewinning book that is now regarded as a classic coming-of-age story exploring themes of racism and prejudice in the 1930s in Alabama, but is also frequently criticized or banned for the use of racial epithets in key scenes. Who is this author? What is the name of this book, which the Museum, Libraries and Archives Council in the UK voted as the one book to read before dying, ahead of even the Bible?

3. Despite her books being the staple of childhood reading

in the UK and outside for decades, this writer was often dismissed as one whose books were 'unchallenging', 'sexist' and 'racist' and her works and any discussions around them were banned on the BBC. Indeed, in 1949 she had to point this out to a BBC employee who was unaware of the ban and had extended an invitation to her for a show. However, despite this, her works are still bestsellers over half a century later. Who is this writer who remains the most widely translated children's author?

4. This author narrates how, while she was on a train that was stuck outside Manchester due to a mechanical problem, she whiled away the time staring at cows in a field outside and the central idea for her story suddenly struck her. The origins of which landmark children's series have been traced to this journey?

5. This children's author had two pretty and talented sisters and, feeling that she was 'the plain one' was also a rebel as a child. She shone in the plays she and her sisters put up and, consequently, she trained as an actress as an adult and spent 10 years in the world of theatre (though she was not very successful). Her time in the theatre and her 'blotting-paper memory' that allowed her to completely relive her childhood experiences, were powerful contributors to the large number of books she went on to write for children. She was stunned at the success of her first book, about three young orphan girls who grow up as sisters. Her third book won the third CILIP Carnegie Medal ever awarded. Who was this author and what was her first successful book (published in 1936 and nominated for the CILIP Carnegie medal), which sparked off a trend, later on, of publishers renaming her

other books so that all the titles ended in 'shoes'?

6. Author and illustrator Eric Carle has written and illustrated over 70 picture books for children. One of these, first published in 1969, has been a phenomenally successful book and has been translated into over 50 languages. The publishers, Penguin Random House, estimated that even five decades later, a copy is sold somewhere in the world every 30 seconds! This book teaches children the names of various foods as its protagonist moves through a series of foods, from fruits to junk food to a nice green leaf, all in one week! What is this colourful tale, which is seen by educators as a metaphor to speak to children about transformations and growing up?

7. '_____land' is named after a popular 1881 children's book by Swiss author Johanna Spyri. It is located in an area called *Bündner Herrschaft*, found between Lake Walen and Sarganser Land, and is an important tourist site in Switzerland. The book narrates the events in the life of a young girl living in her paternal grandfather's care in the Swiss Alps, and many people's idea of Switzerland is inspired by this book. The land and the book are named after the central character. What is the name of the book?

8. The authors of *The Little Baby Snoogle-Fleejer* (1995), *Of Thee I Sing: A Letter to My Daughters* (2010) and *Read All About It* (2008) have all lived at the same address at different points. What address is this and who are these authors?

9. In 2016, the Oxford English Dictionary commemorated the birth centenary of a much-loved children's author by adding some new words coined by him or associated with him, and updating entries for existing words using

examples from his writing. One such term was 'Witching Hour'. Although it first appeared in a 1762 poem, this writer described it as 'a special moment in the middle of the night when every child and every grown-up [is] in a deep deep sleep'. Another new entry referred to 'any of a group of factory workers of diminutive stature', referring to such characters who worked in a very unusual factory in one of his most iconic books. Who was this writer?

10. The books in this children's series by Italian author Elisabetta Dami, published from 2000 onwards, are a huge success in the original Italian as well as in their English translations. Neither the original nor the English versions, however, have Dami's name on the cover as author, instead, the protagonist of the series, a rodent reporter, is listed as the author. Who is this character by whose name this series is known?

11. Michael Bond, the creator of X, died in June 2017. The author had said that this character was partly inspired by all the child refugees he saw passing through stations during World War II, with little tags around their necks. When the writer died, X bounded back into the public eye, especially since a sequel to a 2014 film on the same character was released in the same year. Brexit and anti-immigration tendencies in the UK also led to discussions around the film and books, and an immigration lawyer stated that were X to enter the UK at this point, he would have been denied permission to stay, instead of going home with Mr Brown and finding a family. Who is this endearing character?

12. This author taught English and history for 15 years. He enjoyed making his subjects come alive for students

and when his own son was diagnosed with ADHD and dyslexia, he turned to myths to weave him stories about children who had these conditions and were revealed to be 'demigods'. He had already begun writing books in an award-winning series for adults (the *Tres Navarre* mystery series) before he turned to his children's books, which were a huge success. In fact, the first series he wrote for children was even adapted into two films (about which the author is quite disparaging!). Who is this author who so deftly recreates ancient myths? And who is his first and most famous protagonist?

13. Which country banned the classic children's character Winnie the Pooh, after images of the adorable bear and his friends were used in Internet memes to refer to the country's leader meeting with various dignitaries and the bear was used to represent the leader in other situations?

14. This author was flipping through TV channels one night, passing from channel to channel of reality shows and then a documentary with footage from the Iraq war. She says these images began to 'fuse together, in a very unsettling way'. From this unsettling combination was born one of the most successful dystopian young adult books in recent times, that also went on to become a very successful film franchise. While the writer had written an earlier series, *The Underland Chronicles*, it was this series that catapulted her to fame. Who is this author and what series was this, which was born out of her channel surfing and the myth of Theseus and the Minotaur?

15. Which legendary musician wrote a book called *Gus &*

Me: The Story of My Granddad and My First Guitar? The book tells the story of the bond between the musician and his grandfather, Theodore August Dupree, a jazz musician, who introduced him to music. He wrote the book when he himself became a grandfather for the fifth time, because he wanted to celebrate the relationship between grandparents and grandchildren. The book is illustrated by his daughter Theodora Dupree _____ (the blank being the musician's name) who was named after the grandfather. Who is the writer/musician?

ANSWERS

1. *Madame Doubtfire*; the film was *Mrs Doubtfire*
2. Harper Lee, *To Kill a Mockingbird*
3. Enid Blyton
4. *Harry Potter*
5. Mary Noel Streatfeild (used as Noel Streatfeild), *Ballet Shoes*
6. *The Very Hungry Caterpillar*
7. *Heidi*
8. 1600 Pennsylvania Avenue, i.e. the White House. The authors are, respectively, former American presidents Jimmy Carter and Barack Obama and former first lady, Laura Bush.
9. Roald Dahl; the word referring to the factory workers is 'Oompa Loompa'.
10. Geronimo Stilton
11. Paddington Bear
12. Rick Riordan, Percy Jackson
13. China; the leader was Xi Jinping

14. Suzanne Collins, *The Hunger Games*
15. Keith Richards; his grandfather was Theodore Augustus Dupree

'That is part of the beauty of all literature. You discover that your longings are universal longings, that you're not lonely and isolated from anyone. You belong.'

—F. Scott Fitzgerald

4. ANCIENT LITERATURE

1. The Royal Library of Ashurbanipal in Nineveh (named after the last great king of the Assyrian Empire) is usually termed as the 'oldest surviving royal library in the world'. Nineveh was destroyed in 612 BCE but much of the literature stored there survived the fire that ravaged the library. In fact, experts theorize that the fire actually helped the preservation of the documents. Unfortunately this was not the case at the library at Alexandria, where a huge amount of literature was lost forever. What is the reason for this difference?

2. The Instructions of Shuruppak are dated to be from the early third millennium BCE, making them one of the oldest surviving literature in history. They are meant to teach proper piety, inculcate virtue and preserve community standards. They are supposed to have been enunciated by King Suruppak, who was one of the last kings of the earliest known civilization in the region of southern Mesopotamia (now Iraq). Which civilization was this, which

had literature in the cuneiform script almost 50 centuries ago?

3. One of the oldest deciphered writings of significant length in the world is the Code of Hammurabi. Discovered in 1901, the code is carved into a basalt stele in the shape of a huge index finger 7.4 feet tall. It consists of 282 laws and nearly half of the code deals with matters of contract, establishing the wages to be paid to an ox driver or a surgeon, for example. Written in the now-extinct Akkadian language, it is currently displayed at The Louvre in Paris. The code is named after the king who enacted it. Hammurabi is the sixth king of which dynasty (the region came to be known after this name)?

4. The *Dispute Between A Man and His 'Ba'* is an ancient Egyptian text dating to 2000 BCE. It is in the form of a dialogue where the man accuses his 'ba' of wanting to desert him, of dragging him towards death before his time. His 'ba' describes the sadness death brings and exhorts him to embrace life and promises to stay with him. What is the modern translation of 'ba' from Egyptian?

5. The Epic of Gilgamesh from ancient Mesopotamia is often regarded as the earliest surviving great work of literature. It is dated to have been written in 2100 BCE. The epic poem follows Gilgamesh, king of Uruk, and Enkidu, a wild man created by the gods to stop Gilgamesh from oppressing the people of Uruk. One of the most interesting details is a story about a person named Utnapishtim and how the god Enki commands him to demolish his house and build something. He is then instructed to load certain items, after which the weather

takes a turn for the worse. After this, Utnapishtim finds himself on top of a mountain. What is the natural disaster that befalls Utnapishtim and which other character from another book shares a similar story?

6. This ancient text's name means 'praise knowledge'. It contains commentaries on liturgy, ritual and mystical exegesis in the form of hymns and verses spread over 10 books. The early books that were composed are mostly in praise of specific deities. The newer books also deal with philosophical or speculative questions. Experts believe that the texts were composed around 1700–1100 BCE. Some verses are still recited today during weddings and prayers, probably making this the world's oldest religious texts in continued use. What is the name of this text that is one of the four sacred canonical texts of Hinduism?

7. 'The Book of Changes' from the late ninth century BCE is an ancient divination text and the oldest of the five classic texts of a civilization. It is an influential text read throughout the world, providing inspiration to the worlds of religion, psychoanalysis, literature and art. It uses a type of divination called cleromancy, which produces apparently random numbers. Six numbers between six and nine are turned into a hexagram, which can then be looked up in the book and arranged in a sequence. In which culture's literature is this book found?

8. The Epic Cycle is a collection of Ancient Greek epic poems including the *Cypria, Aethiopis, Little Iliad, Iliupersis, Nostoi* and the *Telegony*. They are all composed in dactylic hexameter and are related to one story in Greek mythology. The story is about a war that originated from a quarrel between the goddesses Hera, Athena and

Aphrodite, after Eris, the goddess of strife and discord, gave them a golden apple. The war was supposed to have taken place in 1194 BCE and there are some scholars who believe it was an actual historical event. The war has provided a lot of content for pop culture and entertainment over the years and the characters are well known the world over. Which war is the Epic Cycle about?

9. This mathematical treatise from 300 BCE consisting of 13 books is a collection of definitions, postulates, propositions (theorems and constructions) and mathematical proofs of the propositions. It is considered to be the most successful and influential textbook ever written. It has been estimated to be second only to the Bible in the number of editions published since the first printing in 1482 which was almost immediately after the invention of the printing press. Till the twentieth century, it was considered something that all educated people had read in their lives. The simple title of the book comes from the Greek word 'stoikheîon' which means 'an essential or characteristic part of something abstract'. Written by Euclid, what is the name of this book that is alliterative when written with the author's name?

10. *Commentāriīdē Bellō Gallicō* (Commentaries on the Gallic War) from 55 BCE is a first-hand account of the Gallic Wars written as a third-person narrative. In it the author describes the battles and intrigues that took place in the nine years he spent fighting the Germanic people and Celtic people in Gaul, opposing Roman conquest. Even though Gaul is used to usually mean France, in this book, 'Gaul' was used in common parlance as a synonym

for 'unsophisticated' as the Romans saw Celtic peoples as uncivilized compared to Rome. Who is the author of this mainstay of Roman history?

ANSWERS

1. Alexandria's literature was written on papyrus scrolls which are highly flammable, and hence were destroyed in the fire. The primary mode of writing in Nineveh was inscribing on clay tablets. These were baked in the fire and hence this potentially destructive event helped preserve the tablets.
2. Sumer or Sumeria
3. Babylon
4. The Soul
5. Great Flood, Noah
6. Rigveda
7. Chinese literature
8. Trojan War
9. *Elements*
10. Julius Caesar

'Only the very weak-minded refuse to be influenced by literature and poetry.'

—Cassandra Clare

5. BIOGRAPHIES AND AUTOBIOGRAPHIES

1. This author's only publication was in 1877. At the age of 14, she fell while walking home from school in the rain and injured both ankles. Disabled and unable to walk, she began learning about horses, spending many hours driving her father to and from the station from which he commuted to work. She wrote her only book when she was an invalid in her house. The novel became an immediate bestseller, with her dying just five months after its publication, but having lived long enough to see her only novel become a success. The novel teaches how to treat people with kindness, sympathy and respect, and is a treatise on animal welfare. Which book is this, narrated as an autobiographical memoir by the titular character that is not human?

2. This gentleman was at one time the second most popular man in England after Charles Dickens. A qualified doctor, he once treated a would-be burglar who injured himself while breaking into his house, free of charge, and then

refused to hand him over to the police, as that would have been a breach of medical ethics. He was revered for his cricket skills, having scored nearly 55,000 runs in first-class matches and taken more than 2,800 wickets. The name of his biography by Richard Tomlinson aptly shares its name with a popular church hymn and is also a fitting description of the man himself. Who was this gentleman and what is the name of the book?

3. David Foster Wallace used to play competitive tennis and once achieved a regional ranking of 17. As he grew older he couldn't compete at the higher levels but his love for the sport did not fade. So he started writing about tennis and even wrote a novel called *Infinite Jest*, in which an elite tennis academy and its students play a key role. In 2016, a posthumous collection of his journalistic essays was released. The title of the book is a clever reference to an integral part of the sport and also to a complex subject. Bill Gates reviewed the book, saying, 'This book has nothing to do with physics, but its title will make you look super smart if you're reading it on a train or plane.' What is the name of the semi-autobiographical book?

4. Helen Prejean is a nun who worked as a spiritual advisor to two convicts before they were executed. After this experience, she was convinced that the death penalty was morally wrong and became a staunch opponent. She wrote a book based on her experience, which was published in 1993. In 1995, this was adapted into a film of the same name, starring Susan Sarandon and Sean Penn. The name of the book comes from a phrase once used in American prisons when guards would lead a condemned man down the hallway. What is the name of the book?

5. *A Prison Diary* is a series of three books (diaries) written by an author who was imprisoned for perjury and perverting the course of justice. The first book is written under the pseudonym FF 8282. Each volume is named after a part of Dante's *Divine Comedy*, namely *Hell*, *Purgatory* and *Heaven*. Each volume corresponds to a prison that he is put in and the length of each volume depends on the time spent there. Who is this author who was once a member of the British Parliament and is also known for his short story collections?

6. In 2016, South African comedian Trevor Noah published a collection of autobiographical sketches from his childhood, growing up in apartheid and post-apartheid Africa. His parents were black Xhosa (his mother) and white Swiss (his father) at a time when interracial unions were illegal and punishable offences. His book pays tribute to his mother's determination that her children should not feel bound by racial stereotypes or oppression and is being adapted into a film that he is co-producing. What is the name of this book, which is a reflection on the circumstances and legal status surrounding his entry into the world?

7. British comedian and writer David Mitchell released a memoir in 2012, which is written as a series of autobiographical musings as he takes a walk around London. He talks about his childhood, schooling and career as a television personality. He also talks about the chronic back pain from which he suffers, also the reason he took up walking in the first place. Given the fact that this book introduces readers to his past and is also a reference to the pain he is going through, what is the

fitting name of this memoir?

8. Gene Simmons is the bassist and co-founder of the rock band, Kiss. The band is known for its members' face paint and elaborate outfits. With their face paint and costumes, they take on different characters. The band has gone through several lineup changes, with Gene being one of only two original members to be there throughout. His autobiography takes a look at the band, the reason they dress up and also the different fights and arguments the members have had over the ages. The name of the book is a neat reference to a phrase which means 'to reconcile after a disagreement' and the characteristic appearance of his band. What is the name of his autobiography?

9. *Born Standing Up: A Comic's Life* is a memoir written by an American actor which chronicles his early life working at coffee shops and clubs as a comedy act, to his eventual fame, and the reason why he quit stand-up comedy altogether at the height of his fame in 1981. The name is a reference to his well-known sense of humour, which he believes he was born with. He is also a successful playwright and banjo player. Who is this actor, known for his frequent Saturday Night Live appearances and his popular reboot of the Pink Panther franchise?

10. This sportsman, who is an American of Armenian heritage, is a celebrated player of his sport and was also known for his appearance, especially his wild hair. When he published his autobiography post retirement, there were several shocks in store for keen fans as he revealed not only that he had used drugs at one point, but also that his distinctive mane had been a wig! The

name of his autobiography refers to the candidness of the book and is also an allusion to the most venerated of the tournaments in his sport. Who is this sportsman and what is the name of his autobiography?

11. Lance Bass quite aptly rose to fame as the bass singer for the American pop boy band NSYNC. He quit NSYNC and formed a production company, Lance Bass Productions, as well as a now-defunct music management company, Free Lance Entertainment. He was also part of a failed mission to put him and his bandmates on the International Space Station. In 2006, he came out as a homosexual. His autobiography, published in 2007, covers all of this and has a three-word name that refers to his band and also means 'working badly; not in agreement'. What is the name of his autobiography?

12. Vic Reeves is the stage name of English comedian Jim Moir who is best known for his double act with Bob Mortimer as Vic and Bob. Known for his surreal sense of humour, he is a regular on panel comedy shows. In 2006, he published the first volume of his autobiography. The name *Me:____* is a neat reference to how he would have originally introduced himself and to the type of book this was. What is the name of this autobiography?

13. *Freedom in Exile* is this gentleman's second autobiography and was published in 1991. His first book, *My Land and My People*, was published in 1962, a few years after he moved to India, where he has been ever since. The title of the 1991 book refers to the freedoms he says that India offers to him. This book was released just two years after the author was awarded the Nobel Peace Prize. Whose autobiography is this?

14. *Sunny Days* is the autobiography of one of India's greatest sportsmen. The book begins with the story of how, for a few hours, he was accidentally switched with another baby after birth and goes on to his debut at the age of 21, when his days in the sun started. The title is a reference to the time he spent on the field playing his game. It is also a neat reference to his nickname. Whose autobiography is this?

15. Corey Feldman is an American actor and performer. He is well known for his multiple teen roles in films such as *Gremlins* and *The Goonies*. In 2013, he published his deeply personal and revealing Hollywood-survival story in an autobiography. The title of the book is play on a word which means 'the sequence of steps and movements in dance' and his name. What is the name of his autobiography?

16. Born as György Deutsch, this man grew up in a Jewish family in Hungary. At the age of 20, he was put in a labour camp which he managed to escape from in six months. However, he lost both his parents at Auschwitz. In order to survive, he hid his identity and joined a pro-Nazi group in which he served for three months before he was discovered. Russian forces liberated Budapest before he could be executed but then he was tried for war crimes because they thought he was an actual member of the group. Eventually, he was let off and he changed his name to George Lang and settled in New York. Over the next few years he got into a field he is best known for, eventually becoming a celebrity. In 1998, he published his autobiography titled *Nobody Knows the Truffles I've Seen* with reference to his troubled life and also to the

field in which he later excelled. In what profession did he become well known?

17. This is a biography of an octogenarian Justice of the United States Supreme Court, Ruth Bader Ginsburg (still serving in the Supreme Court as of 2019). The title alludes to her trail-blazing law career and often radical work. The title is also a slight reworking of the stage name of Christopher Wallace, one of the greatest East Coast rappers of all time, and the inclusion of the initials which the Chief Justice is known by. What is the title of her biography?

18. 'Many things have been written and said about me that I wasn't happy with because they didn't reflect the person I am,' states one of the UK's best-known sportsmen in his autobiography. He claims that many of the controversies generated by his dry delivery of sarcastic wit are chiefly because 'I made mistakes, as everyone does, and then watched, amazed, as they were dramatised beyond all reality.' Who is this sportsperson who was under immense pressure to win a home tournament for his country and finally did it in 2013? What is the name of his autobiography, a reference to the fact that he was finally responding to all the controversies he had generated, as well as a (perhaps unintentional) nod to one of the qualities his game is known for, which makes him a formidable opponent?

19. *Who I Am* is a 2012 memoir by guitarist Pete Townshend. It chronicles his upbringing and the formation and evolution of the band he started. The band is considered one of the most influential rock bands of the twentieth century, selling over 100 million records worldwide. The

title of the memoir is a play of words, referring to their hit single, 'Who Are You?' as well as to the fact of it being an autobiography. What is the name of his band?

20. *Tall, Dark, and Gruesome* is the autobiography published by this legendary actor in 1999. He describes his extraordinary career, acting with stars such as Errol Flynn and John Belushi, his role in everything from animated TV in the Terry Pratchett series and Sherlock Holmes, to playing the role of iconic villains. The title refers to the two things he was most known for, his extraordinary height of 196 cm (6.4 feet) and the dark and gruesome roles he played. Whose amazing autobiography is this?

ANSWERS

1. *Black Beauty;* written by Anna Sewell
2. W.G. Grace, *Amazing Grace*
3. *String Theory*
4. *Dead Man Walking*
5. Jeffrey Archer
6. *Born a Crime*
7. *Backstory* (During the making of this question, the quiz masters discovered that David Mitchell and his long-time colleague Robert Webb started a new comedy series called *Back* in 2017)
8. *Kiss and Make-up*
9. Steve Martin
10. Andre Agassi, *Open*
11. *Out of Sync*
12. *Me: Moir*
13. The Dalai Lama

14. Sunil Gavaskar
15. *Coreyography: A Memoir*
16. Food business; he started restaurants and hotels
17. *Notorious RBG*
18. Andy Murray, *Hitting Back*
19. The Who
20. Sir Christopher Lee

'*The reading of all good books is like conversation with the finest men of past centuries.*'

—René Descartes

6. HISTORICAL AND POLITICAL LITERATURE

1. Hamid Karzai was the president of Afghanistan from 2001 to 2014. He was so obsessed with a certain book, an account of Britain's invasion and occupation of Afghanistan in 1839–42, that he flew the Scottish author to Kabul and spent hours discussing it with him. This information came out through an email that was found in Hillary Clinton's personal email, which she used for official purposes. This book was a work of history rather than fantasy and it won the 2015 Hemingway and Kapuscinski Prizes. Who is this author who is one of the co-founders and co-directors of the annual Jaipur Literature Festival?

2. This adventure novel is about a young man who leaves his home to travel to Paris and befriends a group of people. They have a group of servants who are named after their characteristics. One man was pedantic, generally silent, unsmiling. Another was named after a short carbine, and like a carbine-armed soldier, he was brave and dashing, a

dandy in dress and manner. Yet another was named after the basin that he carried to shave his master, but kept hoping to become a priest once his master changed his career to become one. The last, named Plank, was rather simple in his behaviour. It is a historical novel whose plot exposes various injustices, abuses and absurdities of a time when there was a fierce debate between republicans and monarchists in France. What is the name of this popular novel and these servants?

3. This American writer was born into a political family. As a political commentator and essayist, his principal subject was the history of the United States and its society, especially the way the militaristic foreign policy reduced the country to a decadent empire. His polished and erudite style of narration made his works popular. He fully rewrote the script for Ben-Hur to resolve ambiguities of character motivation for MGM. In April 2019, when WikiLeaks' Julian Assange was carried down the steps of London's Ecuadorian embassy and into a police van, he held a copy of *History of the National Security State* by this author. Name this author who said, 'The people have no voice because they have no information. It could be useful to tell them, actually, what happens around the world.'

4. This socio-political satire was written in Latin by Thomas More and published in 1516. It is a frame narrative primarily depicting a fictional island possessing a seemingly perfect sociopolitico-legal system. He came up with a name for the island from the Greek words for 'not' and 'place', hence the name literally means 'nowhere'. Over time it came into usage in the English language to mean 'a world in which everything and everyone works

in perfect harmony.' The name of the book is the name of the island and it is believed to have invented a new genre of fiction about fictional idealistic worlds. What is the name of the book?

5. This is an alternative-history novel set in 1962, written by an American. It provides an alternative ending to World War II, where the Axis Powers, Imperial Japan and Nazi Germany rule over the former United States. It shows what daily life is like under the resulting totalitarian rule. It even features an alternative-history novel within the novel, where the Allies defeat the Axis Powers. In 2015, the book was turned into a highly successful TV series of which the author's daughter was the producer. What is the name of this novel?

6. This book, a collection of letters giving an overarching history of mankind from 6000 BCE onwards, was written as a guide for the author's daughter. He wrote in the form of letters as he wasn't physically present by her side to tell her this history. It is believed to have been written completely from memory as the author did not have any access to reference books or a library. He wrote about different cultures in detail as he did not like the way history was taught in schools, where it was confined to the history of a single country. Some experts consider it as one of the first attempts at historiography from a non-Eurocentric angle. Who is this author and why didn't he have any access to reference books?

7. *A Connecticut Yankee in King Arthur's Court* is an 1889 novel in which an American engineer receives a severe blow to the head and is somehow transported across time and space to England during the reign of King Arthur. He

uses his knowledge to make people believe that he is a powerful magician but in the end is unable to prevent the death of Arthur. The author wrote this book after being inspired by a dream in which he was a knight himself. This author is better-known for his stories of kids in the American Midwest and by the Mississippi, rather than for stories set in medieval England. Who is this author?

8. This book, by an aerospace scientist and his colleague Y.S. Rajan, examines in depth the weaknesses and strengths of India, and offers a vision of the ways in which India can emerge among the world's top four economic powers and a knowledge superpower by a certain year. The tag line of the book is 'A Vision for the New Millennium'. The name of the book is a reference to the year in which they believe this can happen, and also the standard normal score for the Visual Acuity test which an optometrist might call 'perfect vision'. What is the name of the book?

9. This is a historical novel by Markus Zusak published in 2005. The year is 1939, and the setting is in Germany. The novel revolves around Liesel Meminger, a foster girl living outside Munich, who ekes out a meagre existence for herself by stealing whenever she encounters an object she can't resist and which the ruling powers are intent on destroying. With her foster father's help, she learns to understand what she steals and then shares them with her neighbours during bombing raids. What is the title of the book which describes what Liesel is?

10. *Snow Flower and the Secret* is a book by Lisa See set in China in the 1800s. At that time, women were kept in total seclusion and their feet were bound. The women in one county developed their own secret syllabic code

for communication called Nüshu (women's script). They painted the code on an object that all of them had access to, thereby reaching out of their isolation to share their hopes, dreams and accomplishments. The book is about two girls, Snow Flower and Lily, who seal their friendship through Nüshu. What is this object that completes the name of the book?

ANSWERS

1. William Dalrymple
2. *The Three Musketeers*—Grimaud, Mousqueton, Bazin, Planchet
3. Gore Vidal
4. *Utopia*
5. *The Man in the High Castle*; written by Philip K. Dick
6. Jawaharlal Nehru, Due to imprisonment
7. Mark Twain
8. *India 2020*
9. *The Book Thief*
10. Fan

'Oh! It is absurd to have a hard-and-fast rule about what one should read and what one shouldn't. More than half of modern culture depends on what one shouldn't read.'
—Oscar Wilde

7. PLAYS AND DRAMAS

1. This Russian short story writer wrote to his friend Alexander Pushkin asking for ideas. Pushkin described a case of mistaken identity involving a group of corrupt town officials. This became a satirical play where the characters were given evocative names matching their behaviour. The pompous windbag of a mayor's name had the local words for 'hot air' and 'blow', the judge, reputed for slipshod judgements, is named 'slap-dash'. The warden of charities who bends to the ground is named 'strawberry'. The titular character of the play only arrives in the last scene. Which play is this and who is the author?

2. This play is one of the most popular ones written by this playwright. The plot is heavily based on an Italian tale retold in prose in *Palace of Pleasure* by William Painter in 1567. The use of effects, such as switching between comedy and tragedy to heighten tension and use of subplots to embellish the story, has been praised as an early sign of the author's dramatic skill. This play has

been adapted numerous times for stage, film, musical and opera. In 2010, a version of the play, 'Such Tweet Sorrow', was performed as an improvised, real-time series of tweets on Twitter. The names of the protagonist are so well known that they feature in the NATO phonetic alphabet. What play is this whose story of star-crossed lovers has been retold hundreds of times over the years?

3. The Palais Garnier is a 1,979-seat opera house, which was inaugurated on 15 January 1875 for the Paris Opera, designed by Charles Garnier. Besides being the most expensive opera house, it has been described as the only one that is 'unquestionably a masterpiece of the first rank'. One of the highlights of the building is the seven-tonne bronze and crystal chandelier in the central ceiling. In May 1896, a concierge was killed in an accident. This incident, as well as the discovery of an underground lake, inspired a 1910 novel by Gaston Leroux. What was the accident and what is the name of the novel it inspired?

4. This is a Pulitzer-winning play by Arthur Miller that premiered on Broadway in 1949. It is considered to be one of the greatest plays of the twentieth century. In 2016, an Iranian film *Forushande* won the Oscar for Best Foreign Language Film. In the film, this play is performed by a married couple on stage and the wife is assaulted during the performance. The play revolves around William Loman who tends to reimagine events from the past as if they were real. What is the name of this multiple-award-winning play?

5. The tagline for this play is 'A Trivial Comedy for Serious People'. First performed in 1895, it is a comedy where the protagonist maintains a fictitious persona to escape

social obligations. The play trivializes marriage and satirizes Victorian ways. The title of the play is alluded to many times within the play. At one point, a character says 'one has to be serious about something if one is to have any amusement in life.' What is this immensely popular play and who is the playwright?

6. This is a Pulitzer-winning play by Tennessee Williams which tells the story of a Southern family in crisis, especially the husband Brick and wife Margaret (also known as Maggie the 'cat'), and their interaction with Brick's family over the course of one evening's gathering at the family estate in Mississippi. The ways in which humans deal with death are also the foci of this play, as are the futility and nihilism in some encounters, when confronted with imminent mortality. The name of the play comes from a phrase used to describe someone who is in a state of extreme nervous worry and also refers to a central character and her characteristics. What is the name of the play?

7. This is a musical by Rodgers and Hammerste in which was adapted from the 1909 play *Liliom* by Hungarian playwright Ferenc Molnár. The story revolves around Liliom, who works in an amusement park and whose romance with Julie, a young maid, comes at the price of both their jobs. The play was a failure in Hungary but the 1945 musical adaptation was a huge hit and a particular song from it became an anthem of sorts for a certain football club. What is the name of the musical and which football club's fans sing a song from it?

8. This is a rock musical which is based around Giacomo Puccini's opera *La Bohème* and the life of Jonathan

Larson, the playwright. It tells the story of a group of impoverished young artists struggling to survive in Lower Manhattan in the shadow of HIV/AIDS. Larson wanted 'to bring musical theater to the MTV generation' and he succeeded. The play went on to win multiple awards and ran for a record 12 years. To make the play accessible to the people he wrote for—artists in their 20s and 30s—the production invented the practice of offering daily ticket lotteries before a performance where the winners could buy premium seats at bargain prices. The name of the play comes from the main payment that artists had difficulty in covering every month. Which genre-defining musical is this?

9. This gentleman has the honour of being the first ever person to have been awarded a Nobel Prize and to have won an Oscar. Even today, he remains one of only two people to have achieved this feat. He won the Nobel Prize for Literature in 1925 and in 1938 he won an Oscar for Best Adapted Screenplay for a film that was based on a play of his and has the same name as the play, which refers to a Greek myth. This play was also adapted into a musical under a different name, with the musical going on to become an Oscar-winning film in 1964. Who is this playwright/author and what is the name of his play?

10. This play by Edward Albee was first staged in 1962. It examines the complexities of the marriage of a middle-aged couple when they receive a younger couple as guests and the true relationship of their marriage quickly unravels before their guests' eyes. The name of the play is a reference to a song from Walt Disney's *Three Little Pigs*, but with the character's name replaced by the name of a

popular author. The central characters keep singing this song throughout the play. What is the name of this Tony Award-winning play?

ANSWERS

1. *The Government Inspector* by Nikolai Gogol
2. *Romeo and Juliet*
3. One of the chandelier's counterweights broke free and fell through the ceiling into the auditorium. The novel that it inspired was *The Phantom of the Opera*.
4. *The Death of a Salesman*
5. *The Importance of Being Earnest*, Oscar Wilde
6. *Cat on A Hot Tin Roof*
7. *Carousel*, Liverpool
8. *Rent*
9. George Bernard Shaw, *Pygmalion* (the 1964 musical was called *My Fair Lady*)
10. *Who's Afraid of Virginia Woolf?*

'The purpose of literature is to turn blood into ink.'

—T.S. Eliot

8. POETRY

1. This narrative poem was supposedly based on the true story of a woman's sacrifice to save her lover. It was first published in the August 1906 issue of a British magazine. The poem makes effective use of vivid imagery to describe the surroundings and is reputed be the best narrative poem in existence for oral delivery. The poem was written on the edge of a desolate stretch of land known as Bagshot Heath, where the poet, then aged 24, had taken rooms in a cottage. The poem has been adapted to music to be performed by a choir and has also been the basis of a Hollywood film with the same name. What is the name of the poem and the poet?

2. John Lennon received a letter from a student of his old school, saying that they were analysing the lyrics of songs by the Beatles in their English classes. Quite amused by this, Lennon went on to pen one of the most bizarre songs ever written, just to defy analysis. The name of this song was inspired by a Lewis Carroll poem about two characters. But the character named in the song title is

actually the villain of the poem. Lennon later admitted that the song should have been titled after the other character. The poem is actually recited to the central character in a book, by two other characters. What is the name of the poem and who are the two characters who recite it?

3. This poet and his friend Samuel Taylor Coleridge released a joint publication called *Lyrical Ballads* in 1798, which ushered in the Romantic Age in English literature. After graduation, he spent a year walking around France, Switzerland and Italy, just taking in landscapes and enjoying the natural beauty. He defined his work as 'the spontaneous overflow of powerful feelings'. His sculptor friend Raisley Calvert's generous donation of £900 allowed him to take up poetry full-time. He was Britain's Poet Laureate and his most famous work came about when he and his sister Dorothy took a walk in the Ullswater countryside. When his daughter, Dora, died, he planted hundreds of flowers of the type mentioned in the poem, which to this day can be seen in a field in Rydal. What flowers were planted and by whom?

4. Jalāl ad-Dīn Muhammad Balkhī was a thirteenth-century Persian poet born in modern-day Tajikistan. His works have been translated from Persian into many languages and are still bestsellers in the US. His poems are read at weddings, performed by artists and musicians and endlessly quoted on social media. The 3000-odd ghazals and over 2000 robaiyats (four-line poems) were all written when he was in his thirties or older. The name he is popularly known by refers to the fact that he was from the Roman Empire but it came into use only after

his death. How do we better know Jalāl ad-Dīn?

5. This writer was the first English-language writer to win a Nobel Prize in Literature (also the youngest winner till date). In 1886, he published his first collection, *Departmental Ditties* when working as a journalist for the *Civil and Military Gazette* in Lahore. In 1910, he published a poem full of paternal advice and the lines 'If you can meet with Triumph and Disaster/and treat those two impostors just the same', which adorn an entrance at the tennis stadium in Wimbledon and also the club where the US Open is held. The 'stiff upper lip' self-discipline based culture which is seen in the poem makes it a favourite among the British. Who is this popular poet and what is the name of the poem?

6. This American poet is best known for a poem that is often read at high school and college graduations as a reminder to forge new paths, but he never intended it to be taken so seriously! He enjoyed long walks with a friend who was constantly indecisive about which direction to take and when he finally did choose, often regretted not choosing the other path. His poem 'Fire and Ice' was the inspiration for G.R.R.Martin's epic of the same name and his words 'But I have promises to keep, and miles to go before I sleep... were Jawaharlal Nehru's favourite. Who is this poet?

7. The first non-European to win the Nobel Prize in Literature won it in 1913 for a collection of 103 poems. The original collection had 157 poems but the poet, who translated his own work, did not translate them all. Published under the name *Song Offerings*, this collection is part of the Collection of UNESCO's Representative

Works. Its central theme is devotion and its motto is 'I am here to sing thee songs.' Who is the poet and what was the original name of this work, to which William Butler Yeats wrote the introduction?

8. Rudyard Kipling wrote a poem to highlight the hardships suffered by 20 survivors of a particular battle and the British indifference towards their suffering. This poem is intended to be a sequel to an iconic poem written in 1854 about this battle, which was celebrated for its stirring description of the failed manoeuvre. Indeed, in the poem the survivors approach the famous poet and plead, 'You wrote we were heroes once, sir. Please, write we are starving now.' Kipling changed only one word in the name from a noun (meaning an attack) to an adjective which means 'after all others' or 'the only remaining.' The first poem was written by the then Poet Laureate of the England. What are the names of both the poems?

9. This long poem is regarded to be one of the first ones from British Romantic literature. It is considered to have been inspired by James Cook's second voyage of exploration of the Pacific Ocean. The poet's tutor had been the astronomer on Cook's flagship and also his good friend. According to William Wordsworth, the poet was further inspired when the tutor told him about a book he was reading in which a melancholy sailor shoots a certain blackbird. Who is the poet and what is the name of this poem which is usually studied in school for its usage of personification and repetition to create a sense of danger, the supernatural or serenity?

10. Edward FitzGerald was an English poet who translated

a selection of poems from Persian to English. They are attributed to a certain 'the Astronomer-Poet of Persia'. This poet was famous during his lifetime, not as a poet but as an astronomer and mathematician. FitzGerald's version sold more than two million copies over 200 editions in a few years, making it highly successful. Critics have argued that not all the poems are the poet's and that many of the verses are paraphrased, and some of them cannot be confidently traced to his source material at all. The name for this collection is the Persian word for 'collection of poems having four lines'. What is this work and who is supposed to be the original poet?

ANSWERS

1. 'The Highwayman', Alfred Noyes
2. 'The Walrus and the Carpenter', Tweedledum and Tweedledee
3. Daffodils, William Wordsworth
4. Rumi
5. Rudyard Kipling, 'If—'
6. Robert Frost
7. Rabindranath Tagore, *Gitanjali*
8. 'The Charge of the Light Brigade' (Alfred Lord Tennyson), 'The Last of the Light Brigade' (Rudyard Kipling)
9. Samuel Taylor Coleridge, 'The Rime of the Ancient Mariner'
10. *Rubáiyát*, Omar Khayyám

'At one magical instant in your early childhood, the page of a book—that string of confused, alien ciphers—shivered into meaning. Words spoke to you, gave up their secrets; at that moment, whole universes opened. You became, irrevocably, a reader.

—Alberto Manguel

9. INDIAN LITERATURE IN ENGLISH

1. Padma Bhushan Kallidaikurichi Aiyah_____ is the author of several classic works on Indian history. His most popular work which was published in 1955 is a widely used university text. Unfortunately, his lack of proficiency in his mother tongue has been cited as the reason for his failure to recognize the changing meanings of words over time in his works, resulting in inaccuracies. From 1957 to 1972, he served with the UNESCO's Institute of Traditional Cultures of South East Asia, as the Director of the institute. Who is this author who was described as 'arguably the most distinguished historian of twentieth-century Tamil Nadu'?

2. This is the debut novel of this author and follows the childhood experiences of fraternal twins in Kottayam, whose lives are destroyed by the 'Love Laws' that lay down '...who should be loved, and how. And how much.' This novel came under fire for obscenity in Kerala but eventually was translated into Malayalam as *Kunju Karyangalude Odeythampuran.* There is a Pakistani

television series, *Talkhiyaan,* based on this novel. What is the name of this novel that follows a very unorthodox, non-sequential narrative where the events are not in order? Who is this author?

3. This mother and daughter have been shortlisted for the Man Booker Prize thrice each. The mother is a Sahitya Akademi Award winner and she won a once-in-a-lifetime Guardian Children's Fiction Prize for her book *The Village by the Sea.* The daughter won the Man Booker Prize for her book, rather ironically titled *The Inheritance of Loss.* Who are these two women who have won many accolades in the literary world?

4. This author has authored books in English and Malayalam. His debut work was based on the *Ramayana,* followed by two works on the *Mahabharata* retold from the perspective of the Kauravas. The first of these was on the list of '100 Books to Be Read In A Lifetime' according to Amazon. His books are known for giving voice to the defeated or suppressed. He is currently working on a trilogy based on the blockbuster film *Baahubali.* Who is this bestselling author?

5. S. Hussain Zaidi is a former investigative journalist who started his career working for *The Asian Age.* He has covered the Mumbai mafia for several decades and was doing a story as a freelancer about the torture carried out on the accused of the 1993 Bombay bombings. When the article was published, the editor paid him double the agreed amount on seeing the amount of research Zaidi had done. He continued covering the underworld, cops and the politicians, and in 2002, wrote a non-fiction crime novel that retraces the events that led to the 1993

Bombay bombings and the investigation that followed. The novel was then adapted into a feature film of the same name by Anurag Kashyap with a soundtrack by the band Indian Ocean. What is the name of the novel?

6. Vikram Chandra is the son of noted film and playwright Kamna Chandra. His first novel, *Red Earth and Pouring Rain* written in 1995, was inspired by the autobiography of James Skinner, a legendary nineteenth-century Anglo-Indian soldier. The novel won the Commonwealth Writers Prize for Best First Book. He is best-known for a book that was published in 2006, a cops-and-gangster detective thriller set in Mumbai. It follows the links between organized crime, local politics and Indian espionage. In 2018, a series based on this novel and sharing the same title was released worldwide on Netflix which had episodes directed by Anurag Kashyap. What is the name of this novel?

7. This book by Bangalore-based author Anita Nair is about nine-year-old Siddharth who is the despair of his parents. He does not want to run around or climb trees, and is terrified of ants. Then one day, he befriends a fast-talking, quick-thinking, ultra-intelligent baby elephant called Alise who moves into the neighbourhood. Together the two friends set out on a series of exploits. What is the name of this book which should remind you of the refrain from a popular late–seventies song by the British band, Smokie?

8. This is an English novel written by Paul Harris Daniel who was a medical doctor and had worked in a series of Assamese tea plantations. Published in 1969, it details the terrible experiences of tea plantation workers in the Madras Presidency during the British Raj. The novel

captures the debt bondage of the workers, their poor working conditions and their inability to escape their life. The two-word name of the novel is a reference to the bloodshed of this period, as well as to the different ways of preparing this beverage with or without milk. What is the name of this novel?

9. *The Room on the Roof* is this author's first literary venture. Written when he was just 17 years old, it went on to win the John Llewellyn Rhys Memorial Prize in 1957. The novel is about an orphaned seventeen-year-old Anglo-Indian boy Rusty, living in Dehradun who runs away from his home to escape his strict guardian and to live with his Indian friends. *The New York Times* in its review said,' Like an Indian bazaar itself, the book is filled with the smells, sights, sounds, confusion and subtle organization of ordinary Indian life.' Who is this author who went on to become a Padma Bhushan awardee?

10. Vishwas Mudagal is an entrepreneur. After his internet startup shut down in 2007, Mudagal was on the brink of bankruptcy. He bounced back by writing a bestselling novel and creating a multi-million-dollar company called GoodWorkLabs. The idea for Mudagal's debut novel came from his real-life experience. In the novel, the protagonist also faces bankruptcy but his life takes a turn for the better when he sets off on a journey with Alex, an American hippie. The novel shares its name with an extremely popular song by alternative rock band R.E.M. This Grammy-winning song is known for its main riff which is unusual in that it is played on a mandolin. What is the name of the song and subsequently the novel by Mudagal?

ANSWERS

1. K.A. Nilakanta Sastri
2. *The God of Small Things*, Arundhati Roy
3. Anita Desai and Kiran Desai
4. Anand Neelakantan
5. *Black Friday*
6. *Sacred Games*
7. *Living Next Door to Alise*
8. *Red Tea*
9. Ruskin Bond
10. *Losing My Religion*

Everywhere I have sought peace and not found it, except in a corner with a book.'

—Thomas A. Kempis

10. INDIAN LITERATURE IN THE VERNACULAR

1. *Hind Swaraj*, which can be translated as 'Indian Self-rule' is the name of this 1909 book by a Gujarati writer. It is written in the form of arguments between a reader and an editor. It offers a diagnosis for the problems plaguing humanity and suggests a few remedies. The Gujarati edition was banned by the British on its publication in India, but when translated, they did not ban the English version thinking it would have little impact on the English-speaking Indians' subservience to the British and their ideas. One of the central themes of the book is 'The force of love and pity is infinitely greater than the force of arms.' Who is the author of this book?

2. The 1965 Kannada novel, *Samskara,* about a Hindu society stifled by caste and tradition, is widely considered to be one of the landmarks of twentieth-century Indian literature. Most of the author's works deal with the psychological aspects of people in different situations, times and circumstances. His final book *Hindutva or*

Hind Swaraj, published in 2016, two years after his death, is a critique of the rise of Hindutva nationalism in India, juxtaposing the ideas of Savarkar with those expressed by Mahatma Gandhi. Who is this Jnanpith and Padma Bhushan awardee?

3. This sprawling postmodern epic by Qurratulain Hyder draws on two millennia of history and tells the story of Hari, a monk in post-Buddha India, Kamaluddin, a fifteenth-century Persian thinker, and Gautam, an opportunistic employee of the Raj. The book explores the ceaseless cycles of greed and hate that disrupt the world's beauty. This time-travelling, historical book was written in Urdu and published in 1959. What is the name of this novel by Hyder?

4. This lady was an Indian Bengali fiction writer and sociopolitical activist who worked for the rights and empowerment of tribal people. She has won the Padma Vibhushan, the Sahitya Akademi Award, Jnanpith Award and Ramon Magsaysay Award for her work. Her literary works such as *Hajar Churashir Maa*, *Rudali* and *Aranyer Adhikar* have become classics of Bengali literature. Who is this prolific writer who passed away in 2016 at the age of 90?

5. C.S. Lakshmi is a writer and independent researcher of women's studies. Her works of fiction include *Andhi Maalai* (Twilight*)*, *Siragukalmuriyum* (Wings Will Be Broken) and *Veetinmulaiyiloru Samaiyalarai* (A Kitchen in The Corner of The House). Her work is characterised by her feminism, an eye for detail and a sense of irony. She founded SPARROW (Sound and Picture Archives for Research on Women). Since she uses her real name

for publishing her research work and other articles in newspapers, she uses a Tamil pseudonym to publish her stories. The pseudonym is a reference to a character from the *Mahabharata* who holds Bhishma responsible for her misfortune and, to fulfil her goal of destroying him, she is reborn as Shikhandi (who is responsible for his downfall). Under what pen name does this author write her Tamil stories?

6. This writer and poet was awarded the 1967 Jnanpith Award for his contribution to Gujarati literature. He was once part of the freedom struggle led by Gandhi, where he gained an understanding of history. He eventually became the Vice-Chancellor of Gujarat University. Some of his most popular works are his collections *Hriday Ma Padeli Chhabio* and *Ishamishida Ane Anya* which are character sketches of the literary and historical figures whom he had met. Who is this Gujarati literary giant?

7. Ramaswamy Aiyer Krishnamurthy is a Tamil writer who wrote 120 short stories, 15 novels and three historical romances. His magnum opus is the historical novel *Ponniyin Selvan* which tells the story of the early days of Arulmozhivarman, who eventually became the great Chola King Rajaraja Chola I. This author was better known by his pen name, which was the tenth and last avatar of Vishnu. By what name do we know this author who has a postage stamp in his honour?

8 This eminent cosmologist, who played table tennis with a young Stephen Hawking as a student in Cambridge, is also a noted science-fiction writer. His first foray into the world of literature was when he submitted a Marathi story under a pseudonym for a contest conducted by the

Marathi Sahitya Parishad. He had his wife rewrite this entry as he thought the officials would recognize his handwriting. He went on to win the contest and never looked back. Who is this fascinating scientist and writer, who believes that science fiction must be rooted in hard science, but should have a speculative aspect as well, as seen in the tales of Jules Verne and H.G. Wells?

9. A book by an Odia professor of literature, Akhila Naik, was released in 2008. This novel tells the story of a young Dalit who organizes a resistance movement against a nexus headed by an upper-caste businessman and upper-caste, politically-connected lawyer. This hard-hitting novel has the distinction of being the first Odia Dalit novel and its single-word name could refer to the discrimination or sense of difference that exists between various castes and classes in Indian society. What is the name of this iconic book?

10. *Pratilipi* is an online self-publishing portal based in Bengaluru, which features literature in eight Indian languages: Hindi, Gujarati, Bengali, Marathi, Malayalam, Tamil, Kannada and Telugu. Users can publish and read original works such as stories, poetry, essays and articles and also rate the work of others. The founder Ranjeet Pratap Singh says the name was chosen to reflect the idea that 'you become what you read'. What does 'Pratilipi' mean in Sanskrit (an action usually accomplished on a computer by using the 'C' key)?

ANSWERS

1. M.K. Gandhi
2. U.R. Ananthamurthy
3. *A River of Fire*
4. Mahasweta Devi
5. Ambai
6. Umashankar Joshi
7. Kalki
8. Jayant Narlikar
9. *Bheda*
10. Copy

I know nothing in the world that has as much power as a word. Sometimes I write one, and I look at it, until it begins to shine.

—Emily Dickinson

11. FICTION

1. This successful fiction author won his only Oscar for Best Screenwriter in 1948 for the film *Bachelor and the Bobby-soxer*, starring Cary Grant and Shirley Temple. For the next two decades, he wrote for many TV shows, including creating, writing and producing 'I dream of Jeannie', starring Barbara Eden as a 2000-year-old genie. He started writing the romance novels he is famous for only after the age of 50. After his death in 2007, Tilly Bradshaw wrote a sequel to one of his works. Who is this author who is the seventh bestselling fiction writer of all time?

2. In writing this series, the author was influenced by two murders. Both victims were killed at the hands of men or were victims of honour crime. This systematic violence highly affected and inspired this author to take action against these crimes through his writing. Eva Gabrielsson, his long-time partner, wrote that 'the trilogy allowed him to denounce everyone he loathed for their cowardice, their irresponsibility, and their opportunism:

false friends who used him to advance their own careers; unscrupulous company heads and shareholders who wrangle themselves huge bonuses.' He planned the series to have ten instalments, but due to his sudden death, only three were completed and published. He died in 2004, not having seen the sensation his series became. In July 2010, the series made him the first author to sell a million electronic copies of his work on the Amazon Kindle. Who is this author and what is the name of the series?

3. The following is a line from Honoré de Balzac's 1835 French novel *Le Pere Goriot*: 'Le secret des grandes fortunes sans cause apparenteest un crime oublié, parcequ'il a étéproprementfait.' A paraphrase of this statement in English is found in the epigraph of a bestselling 1969 crime novel: 'Behind every great fortune there is a great crime.' What is the name of this book which is noteworthy for introducing many Italian words to the American audience?

4. *Invisible Cities* is a 1972 novel by Italian writer Italo Calvino. The book is written as a conversation between an ageing emperor, Kublai Khan, and an explorer. The majority of the book consists of brief prose poems, narrated by the explorer, describing 55 fictitious cities. When the emperor asks him to say something about his hometown he replies, 'Every time I describe a city I am saying something about Venice.' Who is this explorer who was also the central character of the book *Livre des Merveilles du Monde* (Book of the Marvels of the World)?

5. This author is one of only three to have won two Pulitzer Prizes. His first Pulitzer Prize was in 1954 for *Fable*,

which was an account of World War I that he personally considered 'the best work of my life and maybe of my time'. The second Pulitzer Prize was for his last book *The Reivers*, named for the gangs of bandits that plagued the Anglo-Scottish border from the thirteenth to the seventeenth centuries. His most popular work though is his 1929 novel about an aristocratic family. The name of the book was taken from a line of Macbeth's soliloquy. Who is this Nobel Prize-winning author and what is the name of the popular book?

6. This Irish satirist and poet has been credited with inventing the words 'modernism', 'truism' and the name 'Vanessa'. His greatest work is a book he titled *Travels into Several Remote Nations of the World in Four Parts, by Lemuel _____, First a Surgeon, and then a Captain of Several Ships*. This book even predicted the existence of two moons of Mars, 150 years before they were discovered. The term 'Lilliputian', introduced in this book, has entered many languages as an adjective meaning 'small and delicate'. This book, which has been made into a 2010 film starring Jack Black, is better known by what name?

7. This author originally called his dystopian novel *The Fireman*. The novel talks about a futuristic American society where books are outlawed and 'firemen' burn any books that are found. The author claimed that he and the editors found the name boring, so they called a local fire station and asked what temperature the paper used in books would burn at. The firemen put him on hold, burnt a book and reported the temperature it burnt at. Which award-winning book is this and who is the author

who used to roller-skate around Hollywood just to get autographs of glamorous stars?

8. In 1928, Hollywood mogul Cecil B. De Mille asked this author to write a script for what would later become the film *Skyscraper*. The original story was about two construction workers involved in building a New York skyscraper, both of whom are in love with the same woman. The author rewrote it with different professions and ended it with the protagonist throwing his head back in victory as he stood on top of the completed skyscraper. DeMille rejected this script and went with the original story. This allowed the author to use these elements in a bestseller about an individualistic young architect who designs modernist buildings. Who is the author and what is the name of the book?

9. This author studied at Cambridge University and then volunteered for the International Red Cross, serving in Egypt. In the early 1900s, he worked as the private secretary to Tukojirao III, the maharaja of the state of Dewas Senior. He wrote about his visits to India in a book called *The Hill of Devi*. He was inspired to write further on the same subject, which led to him writing his most famous book which was published in 1924. This book, whose name is taken from a poem by Walt Whitman, features in the *TIME* Magazines's 'All time 100 Novels' list. What is the name of this author who has been nominated for a Nobel Prize in Literature 16 times but has never won? What is the name of the book?

10. *The Stars' Tennis Balls* is a psychological thriller by Stephen Fry published in 2000. It is a modern adaptation of an 1844 novel. The story revolves around Ned Maddstone

who is the head boy of his school. Barson Garland wants to tarnish his character so he enlists Gordon Fenderman and a friend to do it. Maddstone is eventually locked up in a remote lunatic asylum for years but manages to escape and become wealthy. He takes on the identity of Simon Cotter, an entrepreneur, and plans his revenge. If you were to rearrange all these names, you would get the names of the central characters of the original book. What is the original novel and who is the author?

11. *Gadsby* is a 1939 novel by Ernest Vincent Wright, revolving around the dying fictional city of Branton Hills, which is revitalized as a result of the efforts of the protagonist John Gadsby and a youth group he organizes. The book was little-noticed in its time but is now a favourite of fans of constrained writing and the first editions are highly sought after by book collectors. It even contains Wright's versions of famous sayings such as 'music hath charms to calm a wild bosom' instead of the original 'music has charms to soothe a savage breast', with John Keats' 'a thing of beauty is a joy forever' becoming 'a charming thing is a joy always'. This kind of a book is known as a lipogram. What is unique about *Gadsby*?

12. A 'phalanx' had two meanings in Greek. The first meaning was 'a rectangular military formation composed of infantry armed with spears' and the second was 'a bone of the finger or toe'. This word forms the basis of the name of a cancer-controlling drug in a novel by an American author. The story is narrated by a young girl who has thyroid cancer. The name of the novel comes from a line of Shakespeare's *Julius Caesar*. What is the name of this novel that also led to a highly successful

feature film adaptation?

13. *The Hammer of God* is a 1993 novel by Arthur C. Clarke which deals with an asteroid headed towards Earth and how Captain Robert Singh and his spaceship Goliath voyage to the asteroid with a load of thrusters to set up on the asteroid, hopefully nudging the rock's orbit just enough to push it clear of Earth. The asteroid is named after a Hindu goddess who is seen as the divine protector and the one who bestows moksha, or liberation. What is the name of the asteroid?

14. The name of this place comes from the Latin word for bread. Situated in the Rocky Mountains, it has replaced the North American nations of the twenty-first century at an unspecified future time, after a series of ecological disasters and a great war. The government is a totalitarian dictatorship, a police state in which the outlying Districts are subservient to the Capitol, expected to provide economic goods in exchange for protection. What is the name of this place and in which trilogy does it appear?

15. This novel by Tracy Chevlaier is set in seventeenth-century Holland. It tells the fictional story of a young servant girl called Griet who is called to model for a painting by a painter who specialized in domestic interior scenes. This painter is particularly renowned for his masterly treatment and use of light in his work, which is evident in the painting from which the name of the book is taken. The painting was voted the most beautiful painting in the Netherlands in 2006. What is the name of the book which describes Griet as seen by the viewer?

16. This is a term given to a paradoxical situation from which an individual cannot escape because of contradictory

rules or limitations, as seen in the following example: 'How am I supposed to gain experience [to find a good job] if I'm constantly not hired because I don't have experience?' The term was coined by an American author as the name of a satirical novel that follows the life of a captain in the US Air Force and his men, who attempt to maintain their sanity while fulfilling their service requirements so that they may return home. What is the name of the novel and who is the author?

17. A man had lost his sister to an outbreak of tuberculosis in his hometown during winter. The cold weather prevented the corpses from decaying but the townspeople erroneously came to the conclusion that the dead were surviving on the life of the living, which would explain why the corpses were fresh and the living looked pale. The man was asked to dig up his sister's coffin and to his horror he discovered she was well-preserved. An Irish author was visiting the town at that time and was witness to these events. This inspired him to write a story which would go on to haunt people forever. Who is this author and what is the name of the book he wrote?

18. This novel, first published in 1898, is one of the earliest stories to detail a conflict between mankind and an extraterrestrial race. At the time of publication, it was classified as a scientific romance. One of the most memorable events surrounding this novel was when actor Orson Welles (no relation) read and performed on radio and caused mass panic among the audience who thought it was real news and not a reading of fiction. What is the name of this book that caused such confusion and who is the author?

19. This English author's works frequently appear on bestseller lists and more than a dozen of his titles have been adapted into films. He was initially a reporter for *Reuters* and covered the attempted assassination of Charles de Gaulle, after which he covered stories from Africa for the *BBC*. He wrote novels using similar research techniques to those used in journalism which lent the novels authenticity. He came into prominence when the author revealed in 2015 that he had at one time worked as a spy for MI6. Who is this much-read author?

20. This is a novel by an Australian author who was a convicted bank robber who escaped from prison and took refuge in India. He was known as the 'Gentleman Bandit', because he had chosen to rob only institutions with adequate insurance. He would wear a three-piece suit, and he always said 'please' and 'thank you' to the people he robbed. He was captured in Frankfurt while smuggling heroin and, when in prison, started writing this novel. The book's name comes from the name his best friend's mother gave him, which means 'Man of Peace'. The novel is apparently based on events in the author's life. What is the name of this book which is being developed into a film produced by Johnny Depp?

ANSWERS

1. Sidney Sheldon
2. Stieg Larsson, *The Millennium series*
3. *The Godfather*; Balzac's lines are: 'The secret of great fortunes without apparent cause is a crime forgotten, for it was properly done.'

4. Marco Polo
5. William Faulkner, *The Sound and the Fury*
6. *Gulliver's Travels*
7. *Fahrenheit 451*, Ray Bradbury
8. Ayn Rand, *The Fountainhead*
9. E.M. Forster, *A Passage to India*
10. *The Count of Monte Cristo*, Alexander Dumas
11. The letter 'e' is not used in the entire 50,000-word novel.
12. *The Fault in Our Stars*; the drug is Phalanxifor
13. Kali
14. Panem, *The Hunger Games*
15. *The Girl with a Pearl Earring*
16. *Catch-22*, Joseph Heller
17. Bram Stoker, *Dracula*
18. *War of the Worlds*, H.G. Wells
19. Frederick Forsyth
20. *Shantaram*

'Literature is the most agreeable way of ignoring life.'
—Fernando Pessoa, *The Book of Disquiet*

12. SCIENCE FICTION

1. Frank Herbert, a freelance writer with a feeling for ecology, was researching a story about a US Department of Agriculture programme to stabilize shifting sands by introducing European beach grass. He was intrigued by the idea that it might be possible to engineer an ecosystem, to make green a hostile desert landscape. He published the article under the name 'They Stopped the Moving Sands'. His research however led him to write two short science-fiction novels which he merged and published as one book. It was rejected by more than 20 publishing houses before being finally published by a small publisher. Fifty years later, it is considered by many to be one of the greatest science-fiction novels and has sold millions of copies around the world. Name this novel that was later made into a film starring Sting and featuring music by Toto?

2. This novel was first published in 1968 and is set in post-apocalyptic San Francisco, where Earth's life forms have been greatly damaged by global nuclear war.

The plot follows a bounty hunter who is tasked with killing six escaped robot servants who are like humans, and explores the issue of what it is to be human and whether empathy is a purely human ability. Because of radioactivity on Earth, most animals are extinct, so poor people can only afford realistic-looking robot imitations of live animals. The name of the book comes from a hypothetical situation of whether or not the robot servants could see one of imitation animals when they rested. What is the name of this novel that formed the basis of the immensely popular *Blade Runner* series?

3. 'The Sentinel' is a science-fiction short story written in 1948 for a *BBC* competition (in which it failed to win anything) and was first published in the magazine *10 Story Fantasy* in its spring 1951 issue, under the name 'Sentinel of Eternity'. The story, though initially a failure, went on to change the career of its British author (whose last years were spent in Sri Lanka). It became the starting point for a novel and a film which were developed concurrently. The story deals with the discovery of an artefact on Earth's moon, left behind eons ago by ancient aliens. The narrator hypothesizes that this 'sentinel' was left on the moon as a 'warning beacon' for possible intelligent and space-faring species that might develop on Earth. Which highly successful novel/film was adapted and expanded from this story and who was the author?

4. *The _____ is a Harsh Mistress* is a science-fiction novel by Robert A. Heinlein published in 1966,which won the Hugo Award for best science fiction the following year. It deals with the revolt of humans (criminals, political exiles or their descendants) living on an extraterrestrial object,

against the rule of Earth. They urge various governments to build a catapult to transfer supplies, especially water in exchange for grain. Eventually, Earth concedes and they win their independence. Fill in the blank with the name of the location where these incidents take place.

5. In the 1931 dystopian novel *Brave New World* by English author Aldous Huxley, X is a messianic figure in the World State. 'Our X' is used in place of 'Our Lord'. The World State is built upon his principles of the assembly line—mass production, homogeneity, predictability and consumption of disposable consumer goods. The World State calendar numbers years in the 'AF' era—'Anno X'—with the calendar beginning in CE 1908, the year in which X's first successful product rolled off the assembly line. Who is X and what is the product that, in the novel, corresponds to the beginning of a new era?

6. This is a comedy science-fiction series originally conceived as a *BBC* Radio broadcast in 1978. It was later adapted to other formats, including stage shows, novels, comic books, TV series, video game and a feature film. The novelization of the series is known for being a 'trilogy' that contains five books. The books, though commissioned based on the radio play, have some differences in the script as the author had the habit of improvising as he wrote. Further revisions also had many changes which lead to the situation where all official adaptations and revisions differed between themselves. The author, who was known for his dry sense of humour and love of technology, passed away in 2001 while working on what could have become the sixth book of the 'trilogy'. What fantastic series is this in which our home planet is

described as just 'Mostly Harmless'?

7. The subtitle of this novel is 'The Modern Prometheus' and it was written by a young English author who started the book at the age of 18. The story revolves around a young scientist who conducts an unorthodox scientific experiment. She found inspiration for the scientist's name from an ancient German castle she must have heard about when holidaying on the river Rhine. She wrote the book as a result of a competition with Lord Byron, about who could write the best horror story. Published in 1823, this book is an early example of science fiction infused with elements of the Gothic novel and the Romantic movement. A common misconception is that the titular character refers to the outcome of the experiment rather than the experimenter. What is the name of this novel which becomes very popular during Halloween?

8. This dystopian novel by a Canadian author was originally published in 1985. It is set in a near-future New England, in a totalitarian state ruled by divine law that has overthrown the United States government. This form of government is known as Theonomy where it is believed that the judicial laws of the Old Testament should be observed by modern societies. There is severe limitation of people's rights, especially those of women, making them unable to hold property, handle money, as well as forbidding them from reading or writing. Women are forcibly assigned to produce children for the ruling class of men and the term they are referred to as comes from the biblical story of Rachel. In 2017, a highly successful TV series based on this novel was launched. Due to certain rigid and discriminatory laws passed by the Donald

Trump-led government, women started appearing on the streets in the signature red costumes as a form of protest. What is the name of this highly influential novel and who is the author?

9. Billy Pilgrim is a fictional character from and protagonist of *Slaughterhouse-Five*. This 1969 novel is about how Billy re-experiences moments from various points in his life, albeit without any control over which moments. At various points, he is a prisoner of war, captured by aliens, marries a film star, survives a plane crash and eventually gives a speech to the public where he says, 'If you think that death is a terrible thing, then you have not understood a word I've said.' The author himself was a prisoner of war during the Battle of the Bulge and survived by taking refuge in a meat locker. Who is this author who published an autobiographical collage called *Fates Worse than Death*?

10. This novel, published in 2011, is the debut novel of an author who is the son of a particle physicist and electrical engineer. It was originally self-published as he was rejected by literary agents. He released the book online in serial format, one chapter at a time, free of cost, on his website. On the request of fans, he made an Amazon Kindle version available at 99 cents (the minimum allowable price he could set). The Kindle edition rose to the top of Amazon's list of bestselling science-fiction titles, where it sold 35,000 copies in three months. This led to a publisher contacting him and eventually the published book topped *The New York Times* Bestseller List. A film adaptation was commissioned and released in 2015. Before the film was released, on

5 December 2014, the Orion spacecraft carried the cover page of the manuscript on the first test flight of the unmanned Exploration Flight. What is the name of this book that takes place in the year 2035?

11. This science fantasy novel was written by Madeleine L'Engle in 1962. The story follows three young main characters on a journey through space and time, from universe to universe, as they endeavour to save their father and the world after he goes missing when working on a mysterious government project. The characters are often thrown into conflicts of love, divinity and goodness. The book has inspired a Disney film in 2003 and a 2018 film starring Oprah Winfrey, which was celebrated for its message of female empowerment and diversity. What is the name of the book and consequently the film?

12. Olaf Stapledon in his 1937 book *Star Maker* describes a history of life in the universe. In that, he describes 'every solar system...surrounded by a gauze of light traps, which focused the escaping solar energy for intelligent use.' This concept was taken forward by a British physicist in his 1960 paper 'Search for Artificial Stellar Sources of Infrared Radiation'. He proposed that searching for such structures could lead to the detection of advanced, intelligent extraterrestrial life. Consequently these hypothetical structures were named after him. What is the name given to these structures that encompass a star and captures its output?

13. When former US President Barack Obama wrote about the books he was reading, one particular book stood out. He said that when he read this apocalyptic science-fiction book, he felt, 'The scope of it was immense...because my

day-to-day problems with Congress seem fairly petty, not something to worry about.' This book was the first-ever novel written by an Asian to win a Hugo Award. The book follows Ye Wenjie after she witnesses the death of her father who refuses to denounce the Theory of Relativity. What is the name of this book and who is the author?

14. This 1961 novel by Robert Heinlein tells the story of a human who comes to Earth after being born and raised on planet Mars by Martians. The author got the idea for this book when his wife suggested a new version of Kipling's *Jungle Book*, but with the child being raised by Martians instead of wolves. The working title of the book when he was writing it was *The Heretic* but eventually the title given is a phrase that comes from the Bible in Exodus 2:22. When an inventor Charles Hall tried patenting his waterbed, it was refused on the grounds that it was too close to Heinlein's description in this book. What is this book that significantly influenced modern culture in America?

15. This is the third book in the *Ender's Game* series by Orson Scott Card. The name of the book is a combination of the Greek word for 'alien' and the usual suffix added to mean 'killing of'. In the book, the protagonist switches modes from his acts in the beginning of the series and eventually works towards saving the entire species. What is the name of this book?

ANSWERS

1. *Dune*
2. *Do Androids Dream of Electric Sheep?*

3. *2001: A Space Odyssey* by Arthur C. Clark
4. Moon
5. Ford, Model–T car
6. *A Hitchhiker's Guide to The Galaxy*
7. *Frankenstein*
8. *The Handmaid's Tale*, Margaret Atwood
9. Kurt Vonnegut Jr.
10. *The Martian*
11. *A Wrinkle in Time*
12. Dyson Sphere
13. *The Three-body Problem*, Liu Cixin
14. *Stranger in a Strange Land*
15. *Xenocide*

'Literature is a luxury; fiction is a necessity.'
—G.K. Chesterton

13. DETECTIVE AND HERO NOVELS

1. 'Anagallisarvensis' is a low-growing annual plant that is generally considered a weed and is an indicator of light soils. The petals of the type arvensis are bright red and have flowers that open only when the sun shines, and even close in overcast conditions. This habit leads to names such as 'shepherd's weather glass'. The reason this plant is famous and is featured in a literature quiz is because its common name is the alter ego of an eponymous 1903 play that was later novelized. The protagonist was one of the earliest examples of a costumed hero, and served as an inspiration for heroes such as Zorro, Batman, the Shadow, Green Hornet, Lone Ranger, etc. What is the common name of this plant?

2. Dr Joseph Bell was a Scottish surgeon and lecturer at the medical school of the University of Edinburgh in the nineteenth century. He emphasized the importance of close observation in making a diagnosis. He had a habit of asking his patients a lot of questions about themselves, as well as making observations regarding them. He was

the inspiration behind a famous character created by one of his students. Who was the student and which character was inspired by Dr Bell?

3. 'The Murders in the Rue Morgue' is recognized as the first modern detective story, published in 1841. The author was the first well-known American writer to try to earn a living through writing alone. The Mystery Writers of America present an annual award in his name. His works include short stories, poetry, a novel, a textbook, a book of scientific theory and numerous essays and book reviews. His parents were performing in Shakespeare's *King Lear* the year he was born, leading to speculation that he was named for the play's Earl of Gloucester's son. Who is this author who is better known for his more macabre work?

4. Feluda or Pradosh C. Mitra is a Bengali private investigator who was a big fan of Sherlock Holmes, Bruce Lee and Tintin (just like Feluda's creator). Feluda uses his superb analytical ability, powers of observation (referred to as the magajastra or brain weapon) and sleight of hand to solve cases. Feluda is often accompanied by his cousin Tapesh Ranjan Mitra who serves as the narrator of the stories (like Watson). Initially just books, two of them were made into films by the author himself. Who created Feluda?

5. These amateur detectives are siblings constantly involved in adventure and action. Despite frequent danger, the boys 'never lose their nerve, they are luckier and more clever than anyone around them'. The characters were created by American writer Edward Stratemeyer who was the founder of book-packaging firm Stratemeyer

Syndicate. All the 190 novels were written by various ghostwriters from 1927 to 2005 under one pseudonym. Who are these plucky brothers whose adventures sell more than a million copies annually and what is the pseudonym they can be found under?

6. Although Random House paid a famous personality, known for their work in suspense in Hollywood, to use their name in these books, this person never actually had anything to do with this particular detective series. The books were, in reality, first authored by Robert Arthur Jr. and then by a series of other authors including William Arden and Mary Virginia Carey (with the latter two and several other authors also contributing to another series called the *Crimebusters*, featuring the same trio of teenage detectives). What was the original name of the series and which famous real-life film personality was supposed to play a role in initiating or concluding these mysteries by meeting with the detectives to hear their story or recommending their services to other clients?

7. Tamil writer S. Rangarajan worked in several fields, from engineering (he played a key role in developing India's electronic voting machines) to films (he penned dialogues for a number of successful Tamil films in various genres). He contributed fiction and non-fiction pieces to several magazines and journals, being especially renowned for his pieces that explained scientific facts in accessible terms. Among his prolific output were a series of crime novels featuring the lawyer-detective duo Ganesh and Vasanth. His crime fiction introduced a style that was edgier and more modern than had earlier prevailed, with references to modern fashion, music and with bold

characters. What added to the initial surprise was that these were penned under his wife's name and, until his real identity was discovered, it was thought that a woman had written them. What was this name, under which he continued to write his novels?

8. While 'The Murders in the Rue Morgue' is considered to be the first modern detective story, this book is considered to be the first modern detective novel in English. Indeed, this novel seems to have pioneered, in many ways, the format that so many crime writers used and continue to use, with many people being gathered in a house for an event, including a celebrated detective, and a crime taking place. The events in the book revolve around the theft of a diamond that the English heroine has been gifted by a former soldier in India, who stole it during the Siege of Seringapatnam. The name of the diamond is associated with the Hindu God Chandra and is, interestingly, the name of another gem that is a semi-precious stone. What is the name of the book, derived from the name given to the diamond, and who is the author of the book?

9. The Adventure series written by this Canadian author chronicles the exploits of two brothers who are also budding zoologists. They travel around the world and, unlike their surname, they only capture exotic and dangerous animals for their father's wildlife collection. There are a total of 14 books which travel from Africa to the Arctic. The boys usually start the adventure as a fun trip but end up becoming heroes as they save various kinds of wildlife from loathsome villains. What are the names of the boys and who is the author of this exciting series?

10. This hero was the first fictional character to wear the skin-tight costume which has become a hallmark of comic-book superheroes, and was the first shown in a mask with no visible pupils (another superhero standard). He relies on his strength, intelligence and reputed immortality to defeat his foes. The present incarnation of this hero is the twenty-first in a long line of heroes who have helped Christopher Columbus, Alexander the Great and even met Cleopatra. Readers in India were introduced to this character by *Indrajal* comics. Who is this fearless ghost who walks?.

11. This writer, better known in some spheres for his work as a writer for TV detective shows and for his book series about a teenage spy, was commissioned by the Conan Doyle Estate to write a new Sherlock Holmes story. This is claimed to be the first fully-authorized new Sherlock Holmes story (apart from the authorized teenage series that featured a young Sherlock Holmes). *The House of Silk* was published in 2011 and retains Conan Doyle's original Victorian settings and is also narrated by Dr Watson. In 2014, the writer wrote another book from the same universe, called *Moriarty*, in which Holmes appears only towards the end. Who is this writer, who claims he is not a fan of spin-offs but couldn't resist the temptation to work with this iconic character?

12. This person is the most-translated individual author (103 languages) and is also the world's bestselling fiction writer with an estimated three billion copies sold. The author used to work in a pharmacy during World War I and completed an exam that is usually used to test for an assistant pharmacist. The author's time spent in the

pharmacy doubtless inspired their love for using poisons in the books. Forty-one out of their 66 detective novels contain poisons, unlike detective fictions by other authors who preferred weaponry. One real-life incident involves the author saving a patient's life by destroying an incorrectly compounded drug rather than letting it get into the hands of a patient. Who is this author with a fondness for fatal pharmaceutics?

13. This detective was created by publisher Edward Stratemeyer in 1930. The books are ghostwritten by a number of authors but published under a collective pseudonym. From the time it was first published, the character has evolved and so have the illustrations to reflect contemporary styles. A cultural icon, this character has been cited by various people such as Hillary Clinton, Sonia Sotomayor, Laura Bush and Chief Justice Sandra Day as a formative influence on their lives. Who is this detective and what is the pseudonym under which the series is written?

14. This Scottish crime writer was working towards a PhD in Scottish literature, focusing on the life and works of Muriel Spark, when he wrote his first book about a working-class policeman. He later confessed that he was confused about why this was treated as a crime novel when he had set out to write a modern-day Gothic novel. He thought that the fact that his lead policeman's name was a word for a kind of picture puzzle would have tipped people off to his 'ludic intent'. However, he returned to the character and embraced the tag of crime writing that was given to his books, while reviewers also began paying more heed to the literary quality of his writing,

welcoming him as an important contributor to the genre of literary crime writing. Who is this writer and what is the name of his famous policeman, who still features in the ongoing series (as of 2019)?

15. This author, born in 1940, has penned close to 300 detective novels, most of which feature one of five recurring protagonists. He was an employee of the Indian telecom department when he first began his writing career and his love of crime led him to translate James Hadley Chase into Hindi. When he began writing his own crime fiction in Hindi, he used a variety of protagonists including an investigative journalist and another whom he describes as a 'philosopher' detective. However, of his various protagonists, the most popular seems to be Vimal, an anti-hero with a murky past. Who is this Hindi author whose crime fiction spans multiple decades?

ANSWERS

1. The Scarlet Pimpernel
2. Alfred Conan Doyle, Sherlock Holmes
3. Edgar Allan Poe
4. Satyajit Ray
5. *The Hardy Boys*, Franklin W. Dixon
6. *Three Investigators,* Alfred Hitchcock
7. Sujatha
8. *The Moonstone,*Wilkie Collins
9. Hal and Roger Hunt, Willard Price
10. The Phantom
11. Anthony Horowitz
12. Agatha Christie

13. Nancy Drew, Carolyn Keene
14. Ian Rankin, Inspector John Rebus
15. Surendar Mohan Pathak

'Literature is a textually transmitted disease, normally contracted in childhood.

—Jane Yolen

14. FANTASY AND GRAPHIC NOVELS

1. These two well-loved authors, who had been friends since the early 1980s, decided to collaborate to write a parody of Richmal Crompton's *William* books, named *William the Antichrist*. Each of them wrote their parts, plotted overlong calls and then posted to each other on floppy disks. Because both of them had their own highly successful series of books being published on a regular basis, this book took quite a long time to develop. Eventually, it was published in 1990 and became a bestseller. It is a fantasy comedy about the birth of the son of Satan, the end of times and a mix-up at a small country hospital. The book was adapted into a TV series by Amazon and released in May 2019. Who are these two authors and what is the name of the book?

2. *18 Days*, by graphic novel legend Grant Morrison, tells the story of three generations of super-warriors, meeting for the final battle of their age. It features a collection of short stories revealing new secrets and forgotten tales that led to the epic 18-day climactic war that concluded

the age of the gods and began the age of man. Grant's groundbreaking story is matched perfectly with original illustrations created by acclaimed artist, Mukesh Singh. *18 Days* is Grant's reimagining of which great epic?

3. This manga series was originally meant to be named 'Black' because of the colour of the Soul Reaper's clothes, but the creator Tite Kubo thought the title was too generic. He later tried changing the name to 'White', but he came to like 'X', the eventual title, more for its association with the colour white without being too obvious. The series follows the adventures of a teenager who inherits his parent's destiny and has to defend humans from evil spirits. What is the name of this manga which is one of the bestselling manga in the world and refers to a chemical that whitens?

4. Destiny, Death, Dream, Destruction, Desire, Despair and Delirium are a dysfunctional family of seven siblings who embody powerful forces or aspects of the universe in the graphic novel *The Sandman*. They have existed since the dawn of time and are thought to be among the most powerful beings in existence. They are referred to by a term that defines their characteristics. What is the term by which this family is known?

5. This trilogy by Brandon Sanderson takes place in a world called Scadrial, where the ground is constantly being covered by black volcanic ash fall and every night the land is shrouded in an unnatural fog or mist. The power of magic originates from the two entities 'Preservation' and 'Ruin'. Most people can channel only one of these. A person who can channel both is powerful beyond measure and the title given to this person is the name

of the series. What is the name which is given to those who come out of this darkness?

6. This manga series tells the story of a young ninja whose name refers to a type of fishcake, who searches for recognition from his peers and also dreams of becoming the leader of his village. This is the third bestselling manga series in history, selling 235 million copies worldwide in 35 countries, and makes use of cultural references from Japanese mythology and Confucianism. What is the name of this series which is named after the ninja who has a nine-tailed demon fox in his body?

7. This is a 1884 satire by Edwin Abbott who wrote it (aptly) under the pseudonym 'A Square'. The title is the name of a fictional place where society is built on questionable dogmas such as women believed to be incapable of advanced thinking and prevented from learning to read and write. The novel is a critique of Victorian culture but its more enduring effect is its examination of dimensions which are represented through a narrow viewpoint. What is the name of this novel about a two-dimensional world?

8. Motofumi Kobayashi wrote and illustrated this three-volume manga series about three anthropomorphic rabbits called Botasky, Perky and Rats who fight on behalf of the United States in the Vietnam War against the cats (Vietnamese). Originally, it was published in 1998 in Japan, but when it was released in the US it was renamed to parody the title of a 1979 epic war film by Francis Ford Coppola. The title shares the first word with the film but the second word is replaced by a word that describes the sound that the Vietnamese characters would make. What

is the name of the US version of this comic?

9. This is a major character in a popular fantasy series. He is the only character to appear in seven books of the series. The author often uses capital letters when referring to him because of the evident parallels of this character with Jesus Christ. In one book he even appears as a lamb before returning to his usual form. He is the son of the Emperor-Over-the-Sea. His name comes from the Turkish word for what he is. Who is this character and in which series is he found?

10. This graphic novel series by Frank Miller came about when he was studying samurai ethics while working on *Daredevil*. According to him, the most intriguing character was X, (the title of the series). These were samurai who had lost their master and have something greater than themselves to believe in. Nowadays, the term is used in Japan to mean an 'individual who is without a job or between jobs'. The novel has been credited as being an inspiration for various series such as Samurai Jack, Teenage Mutant Ninja Turtles and films such as *300*. What is the name of this novel?

11. This fictional anti-hero is a blue-collar warlock, occult detective and con man known for his cynicism and snark. He is driven by a heartfelt desire to do some good in his life. This character was created when the artists who were fans of the band The Police, expressed a desire to draw a character that looked like the bassist and singer Sting. In a departure from normal, this character has aged in real time since his creation. Who is this character who was brought to life in 2005 by Keanu Reeves?

12. *Bloodstar* by Richard Corben, *Beyond Time and Again* by

George Metzger and *Chandler: Red Tide* by Jim Steranko were all released in 1976. All of them were designed to be sold on news stands. They were the first to have a certain term printed on them which defined their genre. What was the term that was, for the first time ever, printed on these novels?

13. Belgian Frans Masereel's *25 Images of a Man's Passion* which was published in 1918, is the first such book to be published. It is a narrative style that uses sequences of captionless pictures to tell a story. In the 1970s, cartoonists such as Will Eisner and Art Spiegelman were inspired by these to create book-length graphic novels. The name for this genre comes from the fact that it is completely captionless. What is this genre known as?

14. This is the one of the most successful manga series of all time, having sold 300 million copies worldwide. Written and illustrated by Akira Toriyama, the 519 chapters were printed in 42 volumes and serialized in a magazine from 1984 to 1995. The story was inspired by a Chinese novel *Journey to the West*. It follows the adventures of a young boy who trains in martial arts and explores the world in search of seven magical orbs. This was later adapted into two hugely successful anime series. What is the name of this series which is praised for its use of cultural references from Chinese mythology and Japanese folktales?

15. This is a graphic novel written by Alan Moore and illustrated by David Lloyd that follows its titular character who goes by just one letter, as he begins an elaborate and theatrical revolutionist campaign to kill his former captors, bring down the fascist state and convince the

people to abandon fascism in favour of anarchy. Since its release and the subsequent film adaptation, the signature mask won by the central character has been made a symbol of protest. Anonymous, an Internet-based group, has adopted it as their symbol and every time there is a protest (especially if it is against the government) the mask is prevalent. When asked about it, Lloyd said, 'The mask has now become a common brand and a convenient placard to use in protest against tyranny and I'm happy with people using it.' What is the name of the graphic novel that gave us this mask?

ANSWERS

1. Terry Prachett and Neil Gaiman, *Good Omens*
2. The *Mahabharata*
3. *Bleach*
4. The Endless
5. *Mistborn*
6. *Naruto*
7. *Flatland*
8. *Apocalypse Meow*
9. Aslan the Lion, *The Chronicles of Narnia*
10. *Ronin*
11. John Constantine
12. Graphic novel
13. Wordless novels
14. *Dragonball*
15. *V for Vendetta*

'Literature is strewn with the wreckage of those who have minded beyond reason the opinion of others.'
—Virginia Woolf

15. SPIN THE COLOUR WHEEL

All the books in this section have a colour in their title!

1. This red-haired little girl appeared in print for the first time in a 1908 book. Mark Twain described her as 'the sweetest creation of child-life yet written' and the author went on to write seven more books featuring the lead character and her family. The small Canadian island, Prince Edward Island, that the author loved and where the series is set, is now visited by hordes of tourists, especially Japanese tourists, as the Japanese translation of the book was a resounding success. What is the name of this book and who is the author?

2. This author discontinued his course in architecture and went on to earn a degree in journalism from the University of Istanbul. He published his first novel in 1982 and went on to write several more, all in Turkish. His work is known for its exploration of themes related to Turkish history and identity. Several of his books feature colours in their title: *The White Castle, The Black*

Book and, among his most famous works, *My Name is Red*. In 2006, he became the first Nobel laureate from his country, when he was awarded the Nobel Prize for Literature. Who is this fascinating writer?

3. This 2008 book was penned by a debutant writer and went on to win the Man Booker Prize the year it was published. This author is the fourth Indian-born Booker Prize winner and his book explores themes of globalization and technological change, corruption and caste and identity in India. He was born in Chennai, moved to Australia in his teens with his family and studied at Columbia and Oxford universities. Before publishing his debut novel, he worked as a journalist. Who is this author and what is the name of this book?

4. Alice Walker is an American civil rights activist and a writer who has written many books on racism and the oppression of women in patriarchal societies. Walker had been blinded in one eye in childhood and her mother gave her a typewriter to sit and write with, instead of doing her normal chores. In 1983, Walker became the first African-American woman to win a Pulitzer Prize. What novel was this that earned her the prize?

5. Nathaniel Hawthorne was an American writer in the mid-1800s. He was predominantly a short-story writer, but did write some longer novels in his lifetime. One among these is especially famous and is considered his masterpiece. The novel uses Hawthorne's dislike of Puritanism and rigid social rules, narrating the story of a woman who has a child from an affair and is publicly condemned as an adulterer. The title of the novel refers to the 'A' that she is ordered to wear on her clothes, to

shame her for her adultery. What is it?

6. This book, written by Scott O'Dell, is based on the true story of Juana Maria, 'The Lone Woman of the San Nicolas Island'. The book, which won the Newbery Medal, tells the story of a girl, called Karana, who is left behind on an island when her tribe leaves and how she survives alone on the island for many years until, towards the end of the book, she is found by a ship that visits the island. Scott O'Dell instituted an award for historical fiction, and of all the books he wrote, he is himself perhaps best remembered for the understated power of the story of Karana. What is the name of the book, which is also the name Karana's tribe has given to the island?

7. *Half of a Yellow Sun*, by Chimamanda Ngozi Adichie, won the Orange Prize for fiction in 2017. It is set in the time of the Biafran War, between the secessionist Biafran state and Nigeria (from which Biafra wished to secede). The story is told through the relationships between its lead characters and how their world is affected by the war. Given the central role the Biafran War plays in this novel, it is fitting that its name has a direct link to Biafra. From what symbol, closely associated with the secessionist movement, did the book derive its name?

8. Remi George, better known as Hergé, created an enduring reporter-detective, who travels around the world. Hergé, who had never travelled outside Europe, based his third story starring this reporter in China, after being introduced to the culture and language by Zhang Chongren, a Chinese fine arts student he met in Brussels. In fact, Zhang Chongren executed the Chinese calligraphy seen in the illustrations in this story. What

is the title of this story in which the hero arrives in Asia for the first time and busts an opium ring in China (with one of the subplots involving the Japanese invasion of China)?

9. In 1925, J.R.R. Tolkien produced a scholarly edition of a fourteenth-century poem based on an Arthurian legend. This told the story of a Knight of the Round Table who accepted a challenge from a stranger, dressed in a particular colour. The stranger says they may strike him once with his axe, if the knight who deals the blow then meets him a year and a day later to receive a blow from him. The story then tells of the knight's travels and events that occur during his stay in the stranger's castle, while waiting for the appointed day. While the 1925 edition was not a translation, Tolkien had also worked on a translation of the Middle English text, which was published posthumously by his son. What is the title of this tale?

10. Piper Kerman's 2010 memoir _____: *My Year in a Women's Prison* tells the story of her money laundering and drug trafficking activities, and her subsequent period in prison, describing her experiences and her encounters with other women in the prison. It also served as the basis for one of the most successful online shows produced by a media service provider. What is the five-word title of the memoir (and the TV show), which the writer hoped would allow people to 'think differently about the reality of mass incarceration'?

11. This British author's first fantasy novel for children (part of a three-volume trilogy) won the Carnegie Medal in 1996. Originally released under the title *Northern Lights,*

it was renamed in 1996 and the new name is what has been retained in the film and TV adaptations as well. The books tell the story of a young girl who lives in a parallel world, similar to Victorian England but with advanced technology, who must take on a hostile ruling power, similar to the Church. In 2018, he published the first novel in a new trilogy which features the same character, but at a different age. What is the name of this book, which sparked off a much-loved fantasy series for children, also known collectively as *His Dark Materials*?

12. This 1887 book introduced two characters who would go on to become literary legends in the field of crime fiction, one as the spectacular detective and the other as his friend and narrator. This story first appeared in *Beeton's Christmas Annual* and was one of only four novels written around the central character. The characters enjoyed immense popularity and were written about between 1887 and 1927 (the period which saw the death of the lead character and a grudging resurrection on public demand). What was the title of the book that started it all?

13. This astonishingly successful series started life as a piece of fan-fiction written around characters from the *Twilight* series. The author then reworked the story, changing names and elaborating on situations to create a new series that, when published, was both adored and criticized for its origins and the theme. The erotic novels also inspired a film franchise. What is the name of the series, which is often considered to have made certain boudoir practices a topic of mainstream discussion?

14. This novel was released as a six-volume paperback series

in 1996 by Stephen King, though it was later released as a single volume. It tells the story of a prison in Depression-era America where a warden on death row meets a prisoner with miraculous healing powers. What is the name of this novel, which refers to the name that the prison officials give to the green linoleum strip leading to the electric chair?

15. Judith Kerr is a children's author who has written and illustrated much-loved books for children such as *The Tiger Who Came to Tea* and the *Mog* picture-books, based on their family cat. She has also written a trilogy based on events from her own life, describing how she and her family fled the Nazis and travelled to England as refugees. She decided to share her story when her son watched the film *The Sound of Music* and told her that he now knew what she had lived through! The title of this book refers to a stuffed toy that she left behind when they left Germany. What is the name of this book, which is a part of the required reading list in many German schools?

ANSWERS

1. *Anne of Green Gables*, Lucy Maud Montgomery
2. Orhan Pamuk
3. Arvind Adiga, *The White Tiger*
4. *The Color Purple*
5. *The Scarlet Letter*
6. *The Island of the Blue Dolphins*
7. The element on the central panel of the Biafran flag is a depiction of half a sun.

8. *Tintin and the Blue Lotus*
9. *Sir Gawain and the Green Knight*
10. *Orange is the New Black*
11. *The Golden Compass*
12. *A Study in Scarlet*
13. *Fifty Shades of Grey*
14. *The Green Mile*
15. *When Hitler Stole Pink Rabbit*

'What really knocks me out is a book that, when you're all done reading it, you wish the author that wrote it was a terrific friend of yours and you could call him up on the phone whenever you felt like it. That doesn't happen much, though.'

—J.D. Salinger

16. PRINTING AND PUBLISHING

1. Jubayl is a city in modern-day Lebanon on the coast of the Mediterranean Sea. Around 330 BCE the inhabitants of the city had established firm control over the trade of a particular wetland plant belonging to the family Cyperaceae. So much so, in fact, that the Greeks (the main users of the product) used the Greek name for the city, 'Byblos' to get 'biblion'—from which we get both our words 'book' and 'Bible'. Which is this plant that led us to name our treasured possessions after this ancient city?

2. 'Bibliosmia' happens because of hundreds of volatile organic compounds—acetic acid, butanol, furfural, octanal, methoxyphenyloxime and other chemicals with funny-sounding names. Hints of almond are created by benzaldehyde, while vanillin emits notes of vanilla. Sweet smells come from toluene and ethyl benzene, and two-ethyl hexanol produces a light floral fragrance. What is Bibliosmia?

3. On 30 July 1935, this company published the first

paperback book (*Ariel* by André Maurois). In the 82 years since its inception, the company and its eponymous logo instantly bring joy to avid readers. The iconic logo was first sketched by Edward Young, a 21-year-old office junior who was dispatched to the nearest place to find a 'dignified but flippant' representative of its kind. Currently possessing a slimmer logo and an orange background, which publishing house is this?

4. In Japanese, 'doku' means 'to read'. Voracious readers, the Japanese have words like 'tsūdoku' (read through) and 'jukudoku' (reading deeply) which are in praise of sitting down with a book. 'Oku' means to do something and leave it for a while, and 'tsunde' means to stack things. What is 'tsundoku'?

5. In Bismarck's Germany, quite a few newspapers had this concept of a 'sitz-redacteur'. In one English comic strip in *Captain* magazine, journalists Psmith and Billy Windsor are running a series of articles on a powerful slumlord's misdeeds. Psmith comes up with a brilliant plan, and decides they need a 'sitz-redacteur' if and when they run into trouble. He says, 'We need a 'sitz-redacteur' on *Cosy Moments* (the journal) almost as much as a fighting editor; and we have neither.' Who or what is a 'sitz-redacteur'?

6. This country got its first printing press when a small hand press was brought over with the First Fleet in 1788, but no one knew how to use it. Between 1795 and 1880, a convict named George Hughes taught himself how to use the press and was commissioned by the governor John Hunter to print orders and regulations. In a small printing house behind Government House, Hughes

printed some 200 government orders, several broadsides and a few playbills, including one for a play in which he acted. A playbill from 30 July 1796 is this country's oldest surviving printed document. Which country is this whose history is entwined with the prison system?

7. Johannes Gutenberg adapted an existing press to make the first printing press in about 1439. Having grown up in an area in Germany famous for the product that was made in those presses, he was familiar with the working of the machine. Instead of pressing the usual items, the equipment evenly pressed metal letter forms onto sheets of paper, parchment or vellum. What items were usually pressed and what is the product that would be made in these places?

8. This is the seventh and final novel in a series of books. It was released on 21 July 2007 and brought to a close a series that had started in 1997. It holds the Guinness World Record for most novels sold within 24 hours of release and also holds the record for the largest initial print run of 12 million copies. What is the name of this book which was later made into a two-part film?

9. The oldest printing and publishing house was started with the money from a royal charter granted by King Henry VIII in 1534. It has been operating nonstop since the first pressbook was printed in 1584, publishing over 2,000 books and 150 journals a year across 200 countries around the globe. It also holds letters patent as the Queen's Printer. It is a charitable enterprise that transfers part of its annual surplus back to the university it is a part of. What is the name of this publishing house?

10. Homaro Cantu was an American chef and inventor

known for his use of molecular gastronomy. One of his most interesting inventions was a printed menu card at his sushi restaurant. The paper was made from a mix of corn flour and soy. The menu was printed with ink made of water, glycerine and food colouring. What was special about this menu card?

11. The Bay Psalm Book was published in 1640 by Stephen Day in Massachusetts. One of 11 known surviving copies of the first edition was sold at an auction in November 2013 for $14.2 million, a record for a printed book. What is special about this book's publishing history?

12 Mark Dawson is the author of the John Milton series of novels which is about a disgruntled assassin who aims to help people make amends for the things that he has done. He used to be a lawyer but now he gets his earnings of $450,000 annually from Amazon. Dawson is currently writing three different series. What is different about his books?

13. The Raja Rammohun Roy National Agency is based in New Delhi. As of 2016, it has a website which makes the system faster and more efficient. What does the RRRNA provide which an author requires in India?

14. A colophon is a term derived from the Greek word for 'finishing touch'. The existence of colophons can be traced all the way back to clay tablets from the second century CE. Colophons were formerly printed at the ends of books, but in modern works they are usually located behind the title-leaf. What information would you get from a colophon?

15. This is an American book publisher and the largest general-interest paperback publisher in the world. In

2012, in a £2.4 billion deal, they merged with fellow publishing giant Penguin to combat the growing influence of Amazon and other online bookstores. Most of the recipients of the Nobel Prize in literature have been authors under either label. The company was named so because its founders anticipated just publishing a few books which were chosen without any method or decision. What is the name of this publishing company?

16. In publishing, this is a term given to unsolicited manuscripts that have either been directly sent to a publisher by an author, or which have been delivered via a literary agent representing the author. They are usually read by assistants who, if they find something of interest, can convince a senior editor to run it. The website Youwriteon is a virtual version of the same for various publishing houses. Anthologist John Joseph Adams suggests that the term might have something to do with how manuscripts used to be hand-delivered and tossed over office transoms when the press was closed. When the editors returned, they would then have to wade through piles of manuscripts, just like trekking through mounds of _____y snow. What is this term?

17. This term is used to refer to a person who is hired to write literary or journalistic works that are officially credited to another person as the author. Sometimes the person is acknowledged by the author or publisher for his or her writing services, euphemistically called a 'researcher' or 'research assistant'. What is the term used to refer to these writers that came about because they are invisible to the reader?

18. The Federation of Indian Chambers of Commerce and

Industry (FICCI) since 2014 has been organizing a conference for authors, publishers, librarians, designers and illustrators, content creators, editors, self-publishers, booksellers and distributors. According to a report by Nielsen, there are over 9,000 publishers in India and they estimate the sector is now worth INR 463.53 billion. This conference covers several topics concerning the publishing industry and serves as a platform to figure out solutions through debates and ideation amongst industry think tanks. In keeping with the trend of naming conferences worldwide, what is the name of this conference?

19. THE NBT is an Indian publishing house that came into existence thanks to the vision of Jawaharlal Nehru in 1957. It is as an autonomous body under the Ministry of Education of the Government of India and now functions under the aegis of the Ministry of Human Resource Development. Nehru wanted NBT to be a bureaucracy-free structure that would publish low-cost books.They also publish a monthly newsletter about recent publications. What is the full form of NBT?

20. The gentleman in question was a fiction writer, publisher, illustrator, calligrapher, music composer, graphic designer and film critic. He is the only film personality after Chaplin to have been awarded an honorary doctorate by Oxford University. He designed the cover of Nehru's *Discovery of India* and the logo for an Indian publishing house founded in 1936 in Calcutta, for which he asked for some books as fees for his job. Who is this gentleman and which publishing house's logo did he design (a logo which you will see when you close this book)?

ANSWERS

1. Papyrus
2. The smell of old books
3. Penguin Books
4. Acquiring books but letting them pile up in one's home without reading them.
5. A fake or proxy editor who can go to prison in place of the actual editor.
6. Australia
7. Grapes, Wine
8. *Harry Potter and the Deathly Hallows*
9. Cambridge University Press
10. It was edible.
11. The first book to be published in America (just 20 years after Pilgrim's arrival).
12. They are self-published and available only on Amazon
13. The International Standard Book Number (ISBN) for a book.
14. The place of publication, the name of the publisher and the date of publication.
15. Random House
16. Slush Pile
17. Ghost writers
18. Publicon
19. National Book Trust
20. Satyajit Ray, Rupa Publications

ACKNOWLEDGEMENTS

My love for books and the written word comes from people who probably have no idea how much they have contributed to making my life that much better. First in the list are my grandfather and grandmother, Winifred and Charlotte, who painstakingly built a collection of *Reader's Digest* and encyclopaedias that always surrounded me as a baby. They are followed by all my English teachers, from Vikaasa School, Madurai, including but not limited to: Thilaka Rathnam, Maria Figredo, Sudha Krishnan, Shanthi Mohan, Sita Krishnamoorthy, who introduced me to the world of literature.

BERTY

I grew up surrounded by books lovingly chosen for me, or picked out of their own collection by my parents. I also affectionately recall (and still have) all the books gifted to me by enthusiastic bibliophile aunts and uncles. My school librarian at Besant Arundale Senior Secondary School was instrumental in helping me adjust to a new city and a new school. An internship at Landmark and my stint as a librarian at my university in Durham fuelled and sustained my love for books. I would also like to acknowledge Eloor libraries, Manneys in Pune and the phenomenal Anna Public Library in Chennai as they led to my discovery of so many wonderful books and writers.

AKHILA
We would like to thank the entire editorial team at Rupa for their invaluable help. We would also like to thank our respective libraries and schoolteachers for encouraging us to read and be curious, and our parents, for helping us access a wide range of libraries and reading resources. We would like to put on record our special gratitude to the amazing people of Wigtown, Scotland, for reinvigorating our love for books. Shout out to Akram Baasha, who helped make the newest cupboard to host our ever-growing collection. Finally, we would like to thank friends and family whose shelves we raided and who recommended or gifted us books.

'I was raised among books, making invisible friends in pages that seemed cast from dust and whose smell I carry on my hands to this day.'
—Carlos Ruiz Zafón

www.ingramcontent.com/pod-product-compliance
Lightning Source LLC
Chambersburg PA
CBHW030345030726
47499CB00003B/908